CW00695262

T H E

PRISON

J S W I F T

Cover designed by MiblArt

ISBN: 978-1-7398018-1-6

*For my parents
and your eternal and undying support.*

CHAPTER ONE

A SCREAM OF AGONY ECHOED THROUGH THE ROOM in which Alissa lay. Her insides began to escape through a gaping wound in her belly, slithering to the white-tiled floor beneath her. There was a face, bloated and terrifying as it hung over her, laughing at her pain, and she realised to her horror that the scream had come from her. The life was pouring out of her, leaving a dark, sticky puddle on the floor, and as she started to fade away, she heard someone call her name.

The voice was deep and masculine. With tremendous effort Alissa opened her eyes. It was so dark in here. When did that happen?

Again, the voice called to her from the darkness and slowly her senses began to tell her where she was. There was no tiled floor, it had been replaced by a warm and rather comfortable bed. The harsh florescent lights had gone, and a dim orange glow lit the room, making it feel warm and safe. Instinctively she explored with her fingertips where the wound should have been, but her skin was smooth and unblemished. If Dr Harper hadn't been as skilled as her résumé implied, Alissa would still have a ragged scar from the knife that had been in her torso for less than a minute.

It was no small accomplishment that Alissa had walked away from her ordeal after only two weeks in the infirmary, with no lasting damage. No lasting physical damage.

The voice came again – impatient, demanding, and unfortunately familiar. Alissa coughed, finding her voice after a night of fitful sleep.

'What is it, Garret? What do you want?'

The croak that escaped her lips was barely audible, but that was rectified by N.O.A.H's SmartTec. All voices, no matter how quiet the whisper or how loud the scream, were corrected to an ambient level. Her hoarse voice found its way to Garret and he was clearly not impressed by the implications.

'Alissa, are you asleep?'

'Not anymore. What do you want?'

'There have been some ...' Garret paused; he did that a lot. 'Some problems, in the Rec.' He spoke deliberately, each word carefully chosen for effect. 'I'd get down there if I were you as you are already late for duty.'

The communicator clicked as Garret ended the two-way, and Alissa sighed out her frustrations.

She couldn't shake the queasy feeling in the pit of her stomach, and it had nothing to do with Garret's words. In her subconscious, Silver Glove was a monster – probably something to do with the fact that he tried to gut her less than a month ago – but the dreams about that night were always so much worse than the reality. Alissa pressed the heels of her hands hard into her eyes, trying to push the image away.

Mornings were always the same for her. The visions brought on by sleep were rarely discarded when she woke – they had burned themselves into her mind. The bloated face haunted her waking hours, distracting her, making her feel weak.

Alissa's feet found the soft carpet and she dug her toes in deep. She didn't have time to waste but it was the small things that reminded her of the Complex. Reminded her that she didn't live there anymore. She headed into the wet room. There was no time to shower so a splash of cold water would have to suffice. She stood in front of her mirror wearing an oversized t-shirt. Her ordeal at the Facility had improved her physical appearance massively and she was no longer a chubby mechanic. Their process, while excruciating, had provided her with a lean muscular body and the cheekbones she had secretly always wanted.

Cold water whooshed out of the tap and she cupped her hands beneath it. Once filled Alissa lowered her face into the icy water and allowed the stinging cold to envelop her thoughts. The clarity that this process brought was worth the discomfort. Silver Glove was gone from her mind and instead was the mission statement she had pledged only weeks ago.

The Ark holds us and saves us. We must protect it with Bravery, Compassion and Love. For it is our home and here we belong.

Alissa's thoughts turned to her hair. She had allowed it to grow of its own accord for years and now it framed her face and reached like a dark brown shawl almost all the way down her back. She wrapped it up into a knot and secured it with a band on top of her head.

She hurried back into her room and grabbed her uniform from the floor. Being security chief had not improved her tidiness and most of her belongings had spent at least a day on the floor of her new home.

The black material was tight to her skin and made from a carbon-reinforced fibre that protected her from the majority of known weapons. After zipping the suit Alissa grabbed the belt that housed her gun and communicator and clipped it into place around her waist. Finally, she pulled her boots on while heading out the door, hopping her way down the hallway to the access lift.

The rec room was only one deck away from Alissa's quarters – if she jogged, she could make it there in less than three minutes. The door slid open when she reached it and she walked inside.

She could see that the fight that had broken out was now over. Ordinarily the Rec was a decent-looking place with metallic tables, seats with actual cushions and drinks that tasted rather good. The decor was mostly off-white and gunmetal grey, but it worked for them. People liked it here. Now, however, tables were lying on their sides, spilt drinks and shattered glass spreading across the floor. Chairs had been thrown and Alissa looked disapprovingly at the people in the room. She folded her arms across her chest, a move Garret had shown her. It made you look important. He said that the trick was to remain calm and quiet – people would strain to hear you, and they would be quietened.

The people in the room had split into two groups. On one side was Ryan, from the engine crew. A hard worker but built more for strength than deliberation. Whatever this was about, Alissa would bet that he had started it. Surrounding him were a few of his engineering buddies and three of her own men.

The security detail that stopped the fight had positioned themselves between this and the second group –

three more of her men and two nav officers. In the midst of them, with a tissue pressed against his nose, was Shem, and her heart sank. It was going to be hard to remain neutral in this.

Shem's hazel eyes met her own and she could feel his apology. Beside him was Ham, her oldest friend. He looked scared and Alissa knew why. Ham wasn't a fighter. Of course, he could be, with his large biceps and the extra weight he carried. He would win every time. Alissa often thought that he'd be great on the security detail, but Ham wouldn't hurt a fly.

'Alright folks, I don't care what this was about, I only care that it is over and will not happen again, is that clear?'

'Yes, Sir.' Shem and Ryan spoke in almost perfect unison.

'Good. I need an official report from each of you detailing this incident and further action will be decided from there. Is that understood?'

'Yes Sir.'

'Okay. Now get out of here and let the Rec crew get this place cleaned up. I'm closing it for business for the rest of the day.'

There was a grumble at this from almost everyone in the room. The Rec was one of the few places on board the Ark that was crew only. Now they would be spending their free time fraternising with passengers and civilians. Something the crew hated.

Alissa stood by the door as Ryan and his friends left, followed by her men. They'd make sure he didn't start any more fights. Shem walked towards the door. The side parting in his sandy blond hair was gone, replaced with a messier style that suited him. It was obvious to most that he had copied the haircut from the other nav officers but it looked good with his masculine face; made him look older.

'Come on, we'll go back to my quarters and I'll take a look at your nose. You can fill me in on what happened when we get there.' Alissa's voice was gentle, but Shem knew better than to argue with her.

'Ham, get back to Engineering, your break's almost over.' She smiled as she spoke and Ham nodded and headed in the opposite direction.

Alissa and Shem walked without saying a word. The short journey seemed to stretch out in the awkward silence, and twice Shem seemed about to blurt the whole story out, but he said nothing. He knew very well that once Alissa was in work mode it was hard to get her to listen.

They arrived at her quarters and she opened the door with her thumbprint.

'Welcome home, Alissa.'

The computerised voice belonged to N.O.A.H, the ships computer. Navigation Operations and Habitation. It was one of Ham's best ideas, dreamt up in a moment of brilliance.

Alissa motioned for Shem to sit on a chair in her living space. It was under a light that would allow her to get a good look at his face, and make sure his nose wasn't broken. Ever since she had seen him strung up by the four men something had changed. The image of him, unconscious and helpless, used as a tool to lure her to Silver Glove was burned into her memory. She had promised herself that night that she would protect him forever; indeed, it was probably the main reason she had accepted the job as security chief on the Ark. But there was something more. For more than a moment she had thought she would lose him and the idea of being without him was unbearable to her.

When she had woke up for the first time in the infirmary he had been there, and she had never been so relieved. So why was it so hard to look him in the eye?

He sat in front of her and she clicked the light on above them. It lit his face up and she could see where the blood had dried under his nose. He had been growing stubble, probably because the other guys did. She never thought of Shem as the type to go with fashion trends but here he was, with his new haircut and even newer facial hair. Alissa smiled.

'What's so funny, Al? My broken nose?'

'It's not broken, you baby.' Alissa's tone was playful and felt to her like a glimpse of her former self. A smile spread across her face as she headed to the wet room. Moments later she was back with a damp towel. The blood on his face came off easily enough and there were no other injuries. Alissa sat down in the chair facing Shem and crossed her legs.

'Do you want to tell me why you were fighting with Ryan?'

The business voice was back.

'Not really.'

Alissa raised an eyebrow and stared at her friend in silence. It was a standoff. Neither of them enjoyed the awkward silence, but Shem clearly wanted to keep his story to himself. Eventually, as Alissa stared him down, he sighed and began to talk.

'Well, I was having lunch with Ham. We were on matching shifts and I hadn't seen him properly in days. The Rec was pretty full and when Ryan and his friends arrived there wasn't really anywhere for them to sit.

'There were some seats at our table, so I called them over. Ham had worked with Ryan a couple times and said he was okay.'

Alissa listened intently, nodding as Shem continued:

'At first things were pretty fine. We chatted about work and stuff, but I don't think Ryan was that keen on me. He kept talking about nav officers, how we thought we were better than everyone else. He's just an engineer!'

'Be careful Shem, remember your friends are engineers.' Alissa had learned patience at some point without even realising it.

'I'm sorry, he just made me so angry. He said some stuff that really just …' Shem sighed. 'Anyway, I punched him.'

In that instant Alissa lost whatever patience she had. '*You* punched *him*? You hit him first? What the hell were you thinking?' Alissa stood up and looked down at Shem. 'There is going to be an investigation into this. You could lose your position, end up on the cleaning rota. Is that what you want?'

Shem rose to his feet. At six foot he towered over Alissa.

'I'm sorry,' he said. 'I just lost it.'

'What could possibly make you so angry that you would punch someone?'

'It was Ham.'

Alissa stared at him blankly.

'Ryan was talking about Ham being an idiot. Saying there was no way he could've passed the aptitude test. Said he must be on enhancers.'

'He's not wrong, Shem.'

'That doesn't matter! It hurt Ham, you know, being called stupid.'

13

With a deep sigh, Alissa looked at the ground. 'I get it. There's a good chance I would've done the same. Is he okay?'

'Yeah, he'll be fine.'

Then she felt a hand, strong and warm, gently move the hair from her face and lift her chin. It had been a long time since Alissa had really looked at Shem. It was getting harder to be around him – he was changing with his new job and so was she. It had been a sad moment when she wondered if the two of them were becoming a little too different. He held her gaze for a moment too long and for one brief second, she thought he was going to kiss her.

A voice interrupted the moment, calling her name, and Shem's hand dropped from her face as he took a step back. It was like nothing had happened. Alissa grabbed the communicator from her belt and raised it to her lips, turning her back on Shem.

'Yep.'

'Alissa, I need to see you in my office immediately.' It was Garret. Now she had to be security chief again. She listened for a moment, then turned to look at her friend.

'I have to give a report to Garret. I'll do what I can to keep it off your record, okay?'

She didn't need to tell him that she had to report that he started the fight. Alissa nodded once at her best friend and headed out of the room.

'Get back to work,' she said over her shoulder.

CHAPTER TWO

THE FURNITURE IN GARRET'S OFFICE WAS MADE from a synthesised plastic. It was velvety to the touch but durable – exactly what was needed on a ship like the Ark. Garret sat behind the beige desk in a plush-looking chair that supported his spine in all the right places. It had been programmed by Dr Harper so that as he moved, the chair's structure moved with him, ensuring that he was always at optimal comfort. He didn't like it.

The door chimed to announce a guest and Garret pressed a brightly lit control pad which caused the door to slide open. Behind it stood his chief of security in full uniform. Somehow, she still didn't match the title. All in good time, he thought.

'Come in Alissa. Take a seat.' Garret motioned to a chair on the other side of the desk.

He typed for a moment, looking from the screen to Alissa then back again. Being deliberately slow was definitely becoming his signature move. He could tell that it annoyed Alissa.

Looking at the young girl in his office, he wondered what she had become. Since Alissa had left the infirmary, finding time and reason to pull her from duty had become near impossible. Plus, he supposed, there was a part of him that didn't want to spend time with her anyway. She would always serve as a reminder of how he had been played as a fool by the men in the Facility. How easily he had been led into a plot that might have resulted in the murder of an innocent man. And not just any man – his very own captain. The man he was sworn to serve. He tried to shake the memories away.

The basic training that Alissa underwent during her first weeks as security chief was mostly Garret's design but it was run by others in the field with more hands-on experience in security and safety. The first time Garret met Alissa she had held a gun to his face. Sometimes he wondered if that woman was still here, but in truth he knew that she was gone. What remained was a twenty-five-year-old chief of security who had been thrown into a job she was absolutely not ready for.

'Captain Andover has brought to my attention a situation that he wants rectified immediately.' He kept his voice matter-of-fact. 'A man has gained passage on the ship and the captain believes that he should still be on Earth. It is your job to find out why he is here.'

Garret thought he detected a sigh of relief.

'What's his name?'

'Vincent Stadler. Do you know him?' He tried to keep the suspicion out of his voice.

Alissa answered honestly. 'No, sir. Never even heard the name.'

'Okay then.'

Alissa made it all the way to the door before he stopped her.

'The fight. Can I assume that it is all under control?'
'Yes, sir. Won't happen again.'
'Good. See that it doesn't. Dismissed.'

***

Alissa headed straight to the security office. It was a calm and orderly place filled with screens, each showing a different part of the vast ship. Two women watched their assigned screens, and it was a sure bet that one of them was responsible for Garret's knowledge of the fight. Which, in their defence, was exactly the purpose of their job. Although, really it should have been their boss they informed. Not Garret.

Alissa smiled and bid the ladies good morning. They were coming to the end of a long night shift and looked weary; soon they would be replaced by the next two on the rota. Alissa crossed the room and walked into her little office. There was nothing very special about it. A square room with a steel desk along one wall on which her monitor and control panel sat rather incongruously alongside a framed picture of her with Ham and Shem. Otherwise, just a coat-stand and a metal cupboard. Unlike her quarters, Alissa kept her office spotless. As messy as she could be, she didn't want that to be the impression she gave to her team, who often came into the office to report, or just to vent. The office did make her feel more important than she ever had before. It had become a bit of a status symbol to her, a source of the confidence she had lacked as a mechanic. The plush chair in front of her monitor was probably the most impressive thing in the room and as she settled into it she leaned back, resting her heavy boots on the desk. As always, Alissa was careful not to kick the blank computer screen, albeit it was little used. It was a rare occurrence that she even switched the thing on, much preferring the hands-on aspects of her job to the forms and data.

As she sat, her thoughts wandered. Shem was playing on her mind, likely due to his out of the blue desire to close some metaphorical distance between them. The feeling of his hand on her cheek was pleasant, but inching his face closer to hers? She hadn't anticipated that and wasn't sure if she wanted it. It was fair to say that Shem had an interest in her. He had changed somewhat since they lived in the Complex – had certainly become more attentive. But she couldn't help herself, she had always been dismissive of anything she wasn't prepared for and she often left Shem feeling foolish. For a moment, Alissa allowed herself to wonder how their relationship would pan out. The idea of being with him romantically had never really occurred to her, but would it be such a bad thing? After all, he was her best friend and knew all of her flaws. It could be the perfect coupling, and Ham would be ecstatic. So, what exactly was stopping her from leaping out of her chair right now and running to him? A sense of duty? Fear of ruining their friendship? Maybe she just had to admit to herself that she didn't see him in that way.

The fall from the chair to the floor wasn't a long one, but it wasn't the first time it had happened. Doctor Harper was used to Alissa's frequent trips to the infirmary and was beginning to think of her as a friend.

Groaning, she grabbed for her shoulder, which now hung a few centimetres lower than was normal. The carpet may have looked soft and inviting but it hadn't provided the soft landing it promised. Alissa was sure her shoulder had dislocated. With a grunt of pain she gracelessly clambered to her feet, feeling embarrassingly like her former self – the awkward kid with no grace or poise. She sighed heavily and headed to the medi-bay.

**

As Alissa was falling from her chair, Vincent Stadler was settling down into his. In stark contrast to the security chief, his computer was rarely off. The ambient light from the monitor flashed in his beady, brown eyes as his fingers typed furiously. Sweat beaded just below his greasy hairline and ran into the creases of his furrowed brow. The work he was doing was important and Stadler had vowed to himself that he would not fail his masters. After all, he hadn't been unsuccessful so far.

The keyboard bore the brunt of Vincent's agitation and it fizzed slightly as he slammed a fist onto its plastic keys. It was impossible to concentrate when all he could think about was the night before, and the dream that had burned itself into his memory.

It had started as most of his middle-aged dreams did, with a rich and powerful Vincent who, through the power of his own vile imagination, was devastatingly handsome. Of course, he was surrounded by wenches, riches and delicious food. Dream enhancers were a vital part of Stadler's life, allowing a break from the unfortunate reality that others saw him as vermin, and weren't afraid to say so.

He sat on a golden throne with deep red velvet cushions, in a grand hall whose lofty ceiling was intricately decorated, as though Michelangelo himself had journeyed into the dream realm and presented a never before seen masterpiece. At his feet, Mr Chalmers lay bound, looking up at Vincent with pleading eyes, silently begging for a release that both of them knew would never come. This alternative existence was pure ecstasy for

Vincent; wielding unfettered power was never going to be his path in waking life, but it could be here.

'Vincent Stadler.'

It wasn't a question, it was a demand. It echoed through the hall and the tone was not what he was used to in his dreams. Vincent's eyes darted to locate the speaker.

At the far end stood a girl; early twenties, which appealed to his perverse subconscious. He shifted in his chair, raising a hand on which to rest his chin.

'Yes?' His eyes devoured the long brown hair that fell in waves past her slender shoulders, the muscular frame, the cheekbones and his favourite part of all, the skin-hugging pants that left little to his disgusting imagination. For Vincent, taking in everything about her amounted to sensory overload. This girl was more real than any of the whores he dreamed up and he was dying for a taste of her.

But he found her expression alarming. It was condescension mixed with hatred, something Vincent was accustomed to in real life but not here, not in his own world.

'You don't recognise me?' Her voice was silky, calming. It relaxed him physically and unsettled him mentally.

'Should I?'

The girl's eyes flickered away, as if trying to focus on something that had long since escaped her.

'No, I suppose you never met.'

'Who are you?'

'I am the General.'

Stadler frowned. 'I don't know what you're talking about.'

'I have a responsibility, Stadler, and so do you.'

20

'Responsibility for … what, exactly?' Vincent was becoming unnerved.

'Three years ago, Vincent, you were primed as a potential candidate. You were ambitious, clever and ruthless enough to get what you wanted by stepping on those who got in your way.'

Pride began to swell within him. He wondered if this dream would in fact go the usual way for him, and he shifted excitedly.

'Why, thank you. But what do you mean by primed?'

'One of our agents drugged you, kidnapped you and grafted a tracker into your brain that would allow us to locate you and in due course to make contact.'

The words hung in the air, wrapping around Vincent while his mouth hung open. He waved a hand in front of his face as if to waft away the ominous words presented by his beautiful visitor. His skin became clammy and his throat dried. When he eventually found his voice, he wanted details.

'Who did what to me? When? I don't understand.'

'It was before you fell in with the infernal insurance company. But it doesn't matter now, Vincent. What matters is that the time has come for you to serve your purpose.'

He swallowed hard. 'My purpose?'

'Yes. I need you to finish the job that so many have started. I need you to write a program. One that will cause the Ark to malfunction. Critically. You must take it to the engine room and install it there, directly into the power cells. Destroy the ship and everyone on it.'

'But … what about me?' The question was legitimate but Vincent felt like a fool for asking.

21

'I will save you. I will bring you here, Vincent. You will be a hero in our world. Promoted to work beside me. We will make great things happen.'

'You're asking me to murder everyone on board this ship?'

A deep breath escaped the General's lips as she stepped closer to Vincent. 'The people on board this ship don't care for you, Vincent. Give it time and you will see. They want you off and I believe they will use one of their micro-ships to send you back to Earth, where you will burn with the rest of humanity. Is it really death that you choose? Or glory?'

Those were the last words spoken before Vincent's eyes flew open and he found himself lying on his crumpled bed sheets with an erection he found mildly humiliating.

CHAPTER THREE

DOCTOR MEGAN HARPER WAS TREATING A BROKEN finger in the infirmary, a place of beige, padded walls and medical apparatus protruding over comfortable looking gurneys. Megan's office was at the far end, where double doors led to theatres on either side.

The young man whose finger she was splinting was explaining how he had trapped it in the inner workings of his station while trying to change a fuse. It looked to her more like he had punched someone a bit too hard, but it wasn't her business to say. The accelerated electromagnetic therapy equipment used to set and heal broken bones was relatively new.

Dr Harper held the long, wand-like device in one hand and the man's finger in the other, moving the wand slowly up and down the length of the appendage until the fractured bones knitted together. It was one of many pieces of medical technology that was only available to citizens of the Ark. Back on Earth they still followed the archaic practice of using steel plates and screws to hold damaged bone together until it healed itself.

When the procedure was finished, Ryan stood up and flexed his hand, testing his newly treated finger.

'There will be no lasting damage. You're all set. You can head back to your shift.'

Ryan nodded at the chief medic and walked out without a word.

'You're welcome!' Megan called out to the door. It made her feel better, but the doctor wasn't a fan of confrontation and would have been mortified if Ryan had actually heard her passive aggressive tone. As she was clearing away her tools, the door slid open behind her and for a brief, horrified moment she wondered if the young engineer had heard the remark and returned to give her a piece of his mind. But the familiar groans of an injured party told her this was a new patient. Turning, she saw Alissa standing in the doorway holding her shoulder.

'How many times now?'

Alissa winced. 'Not funny.'

Doctor Harper led Alissa to one of the gurneys and helped her up. It was cool and metallic. Alissa remembered her first time on an examination bed. Her face had been shattered by a chair, held by Captain Andover. She shuddered at the memory.

'How's the captain?' The words tumbled out before Alissa could stop them, and the doctor screwed up her face in response.

'I can't discuss other patients with you, Alissa.'

'Of course not. I just meant ...' What did she mean? That this would have been a good time for Megan to tell Alissa about her relationship with their captain? In truth, it wasn't news anyway – gossip travelled quicker on the ship than a virus through air ducts.

'You two talk a lot. I thought you were friends.' Alissa knew the words sounded empty but if the doctor played along they'd both get out of this without any awkwardness.

A strange friendship had been growing between the two women, filled with awkward moments. Alissa truly owed her life to the doctor and it made her reach out, to extend a hand of friendship that was reserved for just two others. It was good to have a girl to talk to, to share things with. Alissa wondered whether she should ask for help with Shem. Advice about a boy ... Alissa chuckled, them winced again from the pain. After everything that had happened – the violence, the pain – Alissa was no more than a regular girl worried about a boy. The revelation was a happy one, and Alissa clung to it.

'We are friends and if you're asking about Clarke's emotional state, then he's fine.' Megan was gently examining Alissa's shoulder, feeling the contours with her fingertips. 'Okay. There's no easy way to do this. I'm just going to pop it right back in.'

Alissa took a deep breath. She was going to have to be more careful or a dislocated shoulder would be the least of her worries.

Megan positioned herself so that Alissa's arm was resting on her own shoulder; then, firmly grasping the arm, she pulled slowly until the humerus popped back into the shoulder socket. The clinic remained oddly quiet during the procedure – usually there'd be a scream or two from the patient, but Alissa sat calmly with her eyes tight shut.

Megan punched a few numbers into a keypad on the medicine cabinet door and reached inside for a bottle of painkillers.

'Here, take one of these. You'll feel better.' There was a tiny capsule on her outstretched palm.

Alissa opened her eyes, grabbed the capsule and virtually threw it down her throat.

'Thanks, doc.'

'Don't mention it.' As always, Megan's warm smile made Alissa feel at ease.

Doctor Harper was a beautiful woman; if the rumours were true, then the captain was a lucky man.

***

The rest of the day passed uneventfully for Alissa. Much of it was spent in her office trying to find the man called Stadler. Unfortunately for her, the mystery man was nowhere to be found on the ship. The assumption was that he'd spent the day in his quarters – the only place the security crew didn't have surveillance. Ordinarily if there was a wanted man, they would storm his living space and drag him to the prison sector in handcuffs. Unfortunately, this Stadler had evidently broken no laws. It was up to Alissa to find out if his presence on the ship was legal – a nuisance to be investigated – or if he was here under false pretences. In which case it would be a long time in the brig.

The security chief sighed at the monitors and rested her face in her hands, squeezing her palms into her eyes until small glittery shapes began to dance in the darkness like a kaleidoscope of diamonds. The rest of the day would be spent in the company of Shem and Ham. The three of them were meeting for dinner and whilst normally it would be a quiet night at the Rec, since the fight that would unfortunately no longer be an option. They would have to venture out into the noisy crowds of the civilian centre.

The civilian parts of the ship were remarkable. Stone walls surrounded leafy shrubs that sprouted flowers in shockingly bright colours. They were beautiful places to go and socialise and a lot of the senior crew spent their free time there in an effort to avoid places like the Rec, of which the best that could be said was that they were cheap and cheerful. It was possible to walk through gardens filled with heavily perfumed flowers, and to gaze at stars shining through the colossal windows. The food in the civ centre was all organic, grown in the ship's hydroponic department and supplied to the finest restaurants, where it was consumed by some of the stuffiest members of society.

Alissa had seen many pictures and watched the civilian areas on her monitors, but hadn't yet ventured out to experience them for herself.

Putting her workstation on standby, Alissa rose to her feet and quickly grabbed the back of her chair to stop herself falling over from the head rush. Shaking her head at no one but herself, she left her office and headed to her quarters to change.

By the time Ham and Shem arrived, Alissa was ready. She wore black boots over her pants and a dark purple tunic that ended at her thighs. To Shem and Ham, the fact that she wasn't wearing overalls and grease stains was a testament to how much she has grown up in recent months. Shem muttered his approval of her outfit while Ham flung his arms round her. His instructions were strict: no physical contact while in uniform. Alissa felt it was unprofessional. It hurt his feelings, but he understood the reasoning.

Alissa's muscles tightened, a reflex action designed for defence against an oncoming attack. That reflex would never go away. Her reactions had been enhanced beyond her control by the Facility. Taking a deep breath, Alissa raised her arms and wrapped them around her friend. Nothing in the world would ever stop her from loving Ham with all her heart.

'How was your shift today?' The words were muffled by Ham's curly hair.

'Good. The ship is running smooth. Wilkins says we'll be good for years at this rate. Won't need to stop or nothing.'

Alissa smiled and extricated herself from his embrace. 'That's good news because I don't think there is anywhere to stop.' She laughed, but the implication was clear. There was nothing and no one in the vicinity that could help them. If the Ark were to malfunction, they'd be stranded.

'So, where are we eating?' said Shem.

'I don't know but I, for one, am starving!'

***

Doors to the civilian centre were always marked by large signs announcing the requirement for good behaviour and politeness while mixing with the residents. The three friends entered and found themselves in a breathtakingly large area. It was at least ten decks high, with ornate balconies overflowing with ivy whose form and texture contrasted with the sleek white design that characterised the architecture. Alissa didn't know where to look. Every vista was a delight. The entire right side of the area was a window that showed the stars in all their glory. The place was packed with couples walking hand in hand, friends smiling with one another and children laughing as they ran freely around.

The nicest places Alissa had ever seen in New Amerland were shoddy even in comparison with the crew areas of the Ark; against this place, they seemed like hovels.

'This is what Silver City looked like.'

Shem's voice brought Alissa back to herself.

'Really?'

'Yeah, that's why a lot of the crew aren't all that interested in this. They've seen it all their lives.'

Alissa felt a pang of jealousy for anyone who had experienced this day to day. Her own youth hadn't been unhappy, but for a moment she imagined what it would've been like to live in a place like this. It was silly, since now she could spend all her free time here if she chose to. There was no reason to regret the past. But she couldn't help it.

Ham grabbed his two friends, pulling Alissa out of her daydream, and walked between them to a small restaurant at the back. It was dimly lit, and quite cosy. As they walked inside the temperature changed, just a tad warmer, and the walls gave off an orange glow that made it look like the room was lit by naked flames. A girl came over and greeted them with a smile.

"Hey folks, table for three?"

Shem nodded and the girl led them to a round table against the wall, with a cushioned semi-circular bench.

They squeezed in together and the waitress handed them each a menu and smiled as she rested her hand on Shem's shoulder.

'Just give me a shout if you need anything, folks.' It was directed at Shem and he returned her smile as she turned and walked away. Alissa felt a pang of jealousy, then immediately felt guilty. Her emotions had been all over the place since the night in the Facility and it was affecting her daily life. She would need to be more careful with her feelings.

Choosing from the menu turned out to be an event in itself. Alissa had never heard of half the items and her friends were just as confused. Their palettes had become accustomed to fake bacon and toast or cabbage hotpot, but this place used a variety of vegetables and spices to make delicious-sounding meals. In the end, they asked the waitress to bring whatever the chef recommended, and they decided on wine for the table – it would be a novelty after Saime's beer in greasy glasses. Shem had once had champagne, courtesy of Stadler, but he had no way of judging the quality and hadn't tried it since.

The night would be a culinary adventure.

***

As the three friends were placing their orders, Clark Andover was sitting himself down at the glass table in his quarters. It was beside the window, offering an amazing view while he ate. The delivery from his favourite on-board restaurant had just arrived and had been unpacked in the kitchen. The smell of roasted vegetables wafted into the dining area and made his mouth water.

Megan Harper came in carrying two plates. She put them on the table and sat across from the captain as he poured her a glass of wine.

'This really is luxury.'

Clarke smiled at his beautiful companion. 'You couldn't get things like this in New Amerland. You must be used to it on board though.'

'To be honest I've never had the time for luxuries. I was always working, trying to be the best I could. I practically lived off fake bacon and toast. Quick and simple.'

She gave the captain her best smile and he allowed it to imprint itself on his memory. He decided then and there that he wanted to spend the rest of his life seeing that smile.

'She was asking about you today.'

The captain's smile faded. 'Who was?'

'You know who.'

Alissa. Clarke had been trying to avoid the security chief. The thought of seeing her face, the idea that she might expect some sort of friendship from him, was too much to bear.

'Eventually you're going to have to talk to her. She nearly died, Clarke.'

The captain sighed heavily. 'I know, don't forget that I'm the one who kept her alive.' He was the one that treated her in the Facility with a borrowed healing spray. 'But it's hard. Seeing her, talking about it, reminds me ...' He looked away. Clarke had told Megan about his son, how the four men had killed him in an accident along with his wife, and replaced him with a hologram that truly believed it was a child – until it was triggered. Then it became one of them and Clarke lost his son. Megan rose and walked to the captain's side, wrapping her arms around him as she closed her eyes, wishing that she could help him heal.

***

After a veritable glut of good food Ham, Shem and Alissa were merry from the wine, their bellies warmed, as they stumbled drunkenly from the restaurant, causing a commotion when Ham toppled a tray of drinks being carried by the pretty waitress to a table of three girls who were fortunately far enough gone themselves to laugh it off. The hours they had spent in the restaurant had allowed the common area to empty of families, and now it was time for the party animals to have their fun. Which is precisely what Alissa intended to do.

Ham, on the other hand, was looking a little the worse for wear and in no fit state to set the night on fire. Drunkenly he said his goodnights and hugged his friends enthusiastically before stumbling off towards the crew door, which from this side was a lot less noticeable.

Alissa smiled as she watched Ham stagger off and when he was safely through the door she turned to Shem.

'Okay buddy, show me a good night!' The words slurred slightly as they left her lips and she smiled at the sound. Shem laughed and put his arm around her shoulders.

'Come on drunkie, there's a club through the gardens.'

As it turned out, the man who owned the Zone back on Earth had several clubs scattered across the world. He'd also managed to get one on the Ark. Alissa had never been one for clubbing but at this moment she craved loud music and sweaty dancing. As they crossed the gardens the scents invaded Alissa's olfactory senses and she stifled a sneeze, then giggled. In New Amerland she had never experienced fresh flowers, and as it turned out she was a little allergic to them. While Alissa smelt the blooms and sneezed, Shem thought about the last time he had gone to the Zone, and cringed. The girl who had clung to him that night did so out of fear at first and then, once the alcohol started flowing, out of attraction.

32

Sophia with the crooked smile. He wondered what became of her.

They eventually arrived at the big steel doors and
walked inside. The music was loud, repetitive, metallic.
Shem headed to the bar while Alissa wandered onto the
dance floor. Although dancing had certainly never been
her strong suit, she had somehow found rhythm since
the last time she danced. As he watched her, Shem assumed it was something that had happened during the
kidnapping, but he didn't imagine rocking out was a
module the four men taught. His thoughts were interrupted by the sleek and coiffured barman.

'What can I get you?'

'Just a couple of beers please.'

The luxury of ordering actual alcohol that wasn't
served in a grimy glass wasn't lost on Shem, and he sa-
voured every drop. The beers were ice cold and came in
dark brown bottles. Just what they needed in the warm,
moist atmosphere of the club.

By the time he reached Alissa, she was in full swing.
Little strands of dark hair clung to her face and she was
breathing heavily as she moved. Her eyes were closed as
she moved to the rhythm and Shem managed to stand
right beside her without her noticing. With a mischie-
vous smile, he reached out and touched the cold glass to
her bare shoulder. Alissa's eyes flew open and her squeal
was drowned out by the music. Her reflexes weren't
what they normally were but that didn't stop her from
knocking the bottle out of her friend's hand. It flew
through the air and smashed noiselessly onto the wood-
en dance floor.

Alissa stopped dancing and stood there. Composing
herself was hard, and for a moment she didn't know
what to do with herself. She couldn't seem to just relax

and enjoy herself, not when her body could let her down at any moment. Any normal girl would have laughed, grabbed the drink and enjoyed a good night with her friend. Shem, too, was confused and slightly embarrassed by what just happened. The two of them silently started at each other for several seconds, then Alissa turned on her heel and walked off the dance floor and out the door.

She was entering the gardens when Shem caught up with her.

'Alissa, wait. Please! I'm sorry. It was just a joke, I wasn't thinking.'

Shem wasn't to blame and she couldn't let him think he was.

'It's not your fault. It's mine.' Her words were still slightly slurred. Had the two of them been sober, the situation would have diffused itself in seconds, but under the influence it all seemed more dramatic. 'I'm not normal anymore. They made me wrong.' Tears welled in her eyes. She didn't want the words to come out but once they started she couldn't hold them back. And with them came the tears. 'They changed me Shem. They took the bit of me away that I actually liked, the bit that made me … me.'

She looked around her. Because the hour was late they were alone in the gardens. From a distance they must have looked like a drunken couple having an argument.

'Look, I just want to figure out where my place is now. Where this new me fits in. I don't know if I can do that with you so … prevalent in my life. You're different now too. The old Shem would never start a fight, no matter what. And you know that.'

34

Shem felt the cold panic rise within him. He was losing her and he knew it. This was the only chance he would have to keep her in his life. He was barely able to keep his composure.

'Alissa, there is one thing about me that hasn't changed. That will never change. I am in love with you. Completely and with everything I am.'

He reached out and gently lifted her chin. Through the tears he saw her confusion, but only for a moment before his lips met hers.

The kiss lasted a few seconds, enough time for the shock to pass and for Alissa to pull away. Shem realised his mistake as she took a step backwards. Nothing more was said, and Alissa turned and ran out of the gardens, leaving her best friend standing there.

He had never felt more alone.

CHAPTER FOUR

THIS KISS LASTED LONGER THAN THE FIRST. IT wasn't a surprise to her and she allowed him to hold her while their lips danced together. It felt right, comfortable yet exciting at the same time. They should've been doing this from the moment they met.

The cold silver hand ran through her hair giving her goose bumps and making her weak at the knees. This kiss was never going to end, and Alissa didn't want it to.

Then she felt a dull ache in her stomach and looked down to see the knife in her gut. Instinctively her hands wrapped around the handle and slid the blade out of her skin. Blood flowed from the gaping wound and Alissa screamed as Silver Glove laughed ...

Alissa's eyes flew open and she sat bolt upright in bed. Her hand flew to her lips; the taste of Silver Glove was still in her mouth. Disgusted, she dragged herself out of bed and walked across to the wet room. Shaking, she turned on the shower and stood beneath it, still in her nightdress.

The mere thought of Silver Glove caused bile to rise in her throat and burn the back of her mouth. His evilness had filled her in her dream and she had wanted more. The images burned themselves into her mind and she desperately tried to think of something else.

Her thoughts turned to Shem as the water ran down her face. The more her head crashed the more guilty she felt at having left him standing alone in the gardens; though in her defence, Alissa had not expected a revelation of that size to be dropped on her. Alcohol was the devil. She swore to herself that she would never touch it again.

After a few minutes of lukewarm showering Alissa turned off the tap and peeled off her dripping clothes. Wandering back to her room she dried off and dressed for the day.

***

Vincent hadn't slept. Every time he closed his eyes he pictured the woman from his dreams. Everything about her was terrifying yet he was desperate to see her. The decision to try and avoid sleep was probably not his best, but the idea of being pushed to murder was more than he could cope with. For twenty-four hours he had paced in his room; tried yoga using the vid screen tutorial; picked up various books; listened to music; and all the while she was a presence at the forefront of his mind. Exhaustion and hunger were a part of his life now and his stomach ached with a hollowness so intense he thought he might collapse inwards on himself. The feeling was enough to finally push him into venturing out for food. The crew's quarters were basic, with nowhere to prepare food. Unclean and unshaven, Vincent headed out of his room to the Rec.

Upon arrival, he noticed how tidy the place was. Last time he had braved the crowds it had stunk of hard work and made him feel rather queasy. Walking around, Vincent breathed in the clean air and smiled to himself. He ordered water and toast – simple food for his delicate stomach. Finding a seat was easy in the deserted room and he chose the table closest to the window.

He sat, enjoying his quaint repast and the peace that comes with infinite space. His back to the serving bar, he felt completely alone in the vast emptiness before him. It was breath taking. The view distracted him from the sound of the door opening and it wasn't until he heard a voice that he glanced around. His jaw virtually hit the floor when he saw her. The woman from his dream, standing here like it was the most normal thing in the world. Her long hair fell down her back in waves and her face was just as beautiful as he remembered, but without the hardness – this girl looked sad.

Vincent sat staring at Alissa while she ordered coffee. She had her back to the room and didn't notice him at first. As she waited for her order she glanced at her surroundings. A part of her hoped to see Shem, so she could gauge how he was feeling. Instead she saw a wiry, rat-faced man with messy, greasy hair and stubble growing freely on his face, and whilst he had the uniform of a nav officer, he didn't have the full appearance. Alissa could feel his eyes burning into her, unblinking, and it made her feel uneasy. Turning away, she pulled out her comms pad.

'Noah,' she said quietly, 'can you please show me a picture of Vincent Stadler?'

A face popped up. He looked better, cleaner, but glancing between the two it was clear as day that this was the man she was searching for.

Picking up her hot cup, Alissa crossed the room and sat at the table with the pointy-faced man. His eyes never left her as she crossed the room and it unsettled her deeply. She felt violated, almost devoured.

The hard seat offered little comfort as she sat down beside Vincent. His eyes had finally left her and were staring into the black. If this woman was real, then the woman in the dream must be real. Was this the push he needed? Seeing the vision from his own dream sitting right beside him concentrated his mind.

'I have some questions for you, Mr Stadler.' Alissa was using her best professional voice. This conversation would be led by her. There was no response, so she continued: 'You had explicit instructions not to board this ship. From the captain's own lips. How did you get on the manifest?'

Vincent slowly turned his face towards her.

'I am supposed to be here. I work here.' His voice was quiet, heavy with exhaustion. 'I was offered this position by a chief nav officer. If you want me off this ship, you'll have to talk to him.'

'Fine. What is his name?'

'Mitchell. Shem Mitchell.'

***

Alissa slammed her palms onto Garrett's immaculate desk and leant in to face him. Her mind was racing. She was angry with Shem for his stupidity but more so with Garret. He would've known exactly who had added Vincent to the manifest but what she didn't understand was why he'd given her this job.

Garrett's expression never changed. He simply met her glare and held it until Alissa looked away. Defeated, at least for the moment, she sat in the chair facing his desk.

'Why'd you send me after him? Who is he?'

'That's the problem, Alissa. We don't know.' He was choosing his words carefully. 'What we do know is that Mr Mitchell offered him the position. We have confirmed that much. What Mitchell wouldn't tell us is what led him to make that decision.'

'You want me to find out?'

'He trusts you. The two of you are close. I need to know Stadler's intentions on board this ship and I need to know if anyone is working with him. This is a ... delicate operation, Alissa. You will need tact and diplomacy.'

Alissa took a deep breath. 'What happens to Shem?'

'That depends entirely on the information you gather.'

Alissa rose to her feet. She could feel her heart pounding but wasn't going to let Garrett see her upset. As the door to his office slid closed behind her, she let out her breath in a long whoosh. She didn't really want to see Shem. Not yet anyway. A chance meeting was one thing but to actively seek him out? It wasn't going to be easy. Their awkward encounter was less than eight hours ago and probably still quite fresh in his mind.

Alissa repeated the ships mission statement to herself as she walked along the hallway to Shem's quarters. Today was not going to be a good day.

CHAPTER FIVE

THE AIR SMELT STALE, AS THOUGH THE DEAD HAD rested here until they decayed into dust centuries ago. Vincent held his hand over his nostrils in a vain attempt to keep out the stink, his watery eyes searching his surroundings for some semblance of familiarity. Mostly he looked for Alissa, as she was known on board the Ark. How could the General inhabit her body?

There was no one here. The room was dark and dank – the fetid atmosphere depressed him beyond words. He pondered how easy it would be to curl up here and give up on life. The very air he was breathing seemed to take away any remaining enthusiasm for his life on the Ark. It was an unsettling feeling since he had begun to look forward to his future with the General.

Vincent's eyes began to adjust to the dark and he could make out the outline of a door. It was old-fashioned, different to what he was used to. He turned the metal knob and the door swung open rather than sliding sideways, to reveal a wide corridor, lit only by

41

flaming wooden torches, that matched the room in its foreboding presence. How had he ended up in this place? Thinking hard, he realised he had no recollection of his journey here and yet his ignorance didn't concern him. There was an odd feeling of belonging. The General was here somewhere. He knew it.

The corridor seemed to stretch interminably into the darkness, and as he walked Vincent began to tire. There were no other doors, no corridors intersecting or leading off. Vincent had no choice but to continue on his way and hope to see her. What would life be like after the Ark? Vincent's thoughts took him far ahead. He pictured a world where he was a human alone in a sea of alien life. From one point of view, he had to admit it was exactly what he was looking for – an escape from stronger, better-looking, more intelligent men. When he was the last human alive, he would be the best by default. His thin lips twisted into a wicked smile and he straightened up, walking as proudly as he dared.

The footsteps were faint at first, echoing his own, so in sync that he somehow failed to grasp that he wasn't alone. Until the hand reached for his shoulder and firmly gripped him from behind, stopping him in his tracks. Vincent screamed – a high-pitched, feminine sound that hadn't escaped his lips since childhood. He recovered himself and turned, almost spitting with anger, to face the man who had humiliated him so easily.

He found himself face to face with the General.

As usual she looked radiantly beautiful. His middle-aged eyes immediately found their way to her chest and stayed there until her hard voice interrupted his thoughts.

'Vincent.'

The sound that came out of her mouth didn't match her face. It was harsh and felt like it was scratching the inside of Vincent's brain. It made him feel weak and dizzy.

'Where am I?' he said, almost whispering.

'You're on my ship, Vincent.'

'How ... how did I get here?' Vincent's voice was becoming shaky. Was it possible he had travelled across the galaxy to wherever the General called home?

'You're not really here Vincent. Your image is being projected along with mine.'

It all seemed so real that Vincent couldn't be certain of anything. He had smelled the stench of fear and death in the air. He was afraid of this woman and wanted to please her; he had no wish to feel her wrath.

'Vincent. They are looking for you.'

The warning was obvious by the tone of voice. Had he displeased her? The plan was still in place and going well, he thought.

'They suspect you of something, but they don't yet know the extent of our agreement. You must begin your work, Vincent, and complete it before they stop you. Because you see, if you are unsuccessful you may find yourself in this place, locked away for the rest of your existence, and while you beg for freedom from the pain and torture you will find me unsympathetic to your plight.'

Vincent blinked hard and beads of panic sweat began to form on his sharply sloping forehead.

'I won't let you down,' he said. 'I'll destroy the ship. I swear to you.'

The General nodded her head and turned to leave. As she walked away the hallway began to fade. Vincent's vision was turning black, and in a panic he rubbed his eyes hard. When he opened them again, he was back in his tiny room on board the ship, feeling just as exhausted as before he went to sleep. He sighed, got out of bed and headed back to his terminal to begin work.

He spent many hours trawling through literature on the nature of computer viruses and how they affected the equipment on which they were installed. When he began writing the scripts it became clear to Vincent that he would need to test the results a few times to ensure that the whole thing would work. He looked at non-essential, isolated parts of the ship that he could infect. It had to be perfect – one mistake and the   General would never forgive him.

***

The rubber soles on her boots made no sound in the carpeted corridors. Shem's door appeared in front of her all too soon. Why couldn't it have taken longer to get here? Maybe then she would have thought of something to say. Taking a deep breath, she pressed the call button, and Shem opened the door.

'Alissa! I wasn't expecting to see you here. Not that it's a bad thing, I just thought you were mad at me.' For a moment Shem felt hopeful, but Alissa's silence, coupled with her lack of eye contact, worried him. 'Look, about last night. I—'

Alissa raised a hand.

'I'm not here about that.' Her words were spoken quietly, and it occurred to Shem that he had never seen her look so unhappy. He stepped aside and motioned her through the door.

'Shem, what do you know about a man named Vincent Stadler?'

Still no eye contact.

'Why are you asking me that?'

Alissa's stomach sank. 'Why are you avoiding the question?'

Shem sighed and sank onto the chair behind him. 'I hired him.'

'Why?' Her voice was pleading.

'Because I thought he would be a good candidate for the job and ... If I hadn't, he would've been left on Earth to die. I didn't want that on my conscience.'

'Did you get his test scores? Put together an application portfolio?'

Shem shook his head and looked at the floor. Alissa crouched in front of him and gently lifted his chin with her fingertips until their eyes finally met.

'They're looking for him,' she said. 'The captain and Garret. They think he should still be on Earth and want to know why you let him on board. I don't know how much I can help you with this, but I'll be with you no matter what. You just need to tell me exactly what happened. Okay?'

Shem nodded his head miserably as he spoke. He relayed the entire story of the night he spent with Stadler in the Zone. Alissa flinched when he told her about the grisly death of the bald man that was accompanying them through the tunnel, and she looked worried when he explained how Stadler had killed one of the Unpleasant Ones.

'He saved us that night. I thought he was a hero. I thought that when the captain found out I'd recruited someone so experienced he'd be pleased with me.'

Alissa sat silently through the tale, absorbing every detail, hoping to understand the reason for the captain's suspicions. The ending left her confused. Technically,

45

Shem had done nothing wrong. There was paperwork that needed filling in, registration documents and so forth, to get someone checked and added to the crew's manifest. Stadler was listed temporarily with a view to permanency when the paperwork went through. This was not unusual and would normally be done on Earth, but with time being short Shem had decided to complete the required papers while on board.

It was certainly the way of things on short-term missions. You headed back to Earth regularly and if there were major problems people could be offloaded once you returned. The problem was, this ship wasn't going back; once on board there was no option to leave. If this man turned out to be dangerous, then he and Shem could both end up in the brig.

Alissa sucked in a deep breath and held it for a few seconds while she put her thoughts in order. Shem watched her in silence and whilst he was mostly worried about his job on board the ship, there was a small part of him that was thinking about the irreparable damage he may have caused to their friendship. Shem's eyes roamed over Alissa's face, memorising every detail. He was taking her all in, concerned that he might never see her beyond the context of work again.

Alissa opened her eyes and steeled herself. She had made her decision and now she had to break it to Shem.

'I know you, and I don't believe that you had malicious intent bringing Vincent Stadler on board. I believe he is manipulative and used your trusting nature to ensure his own survival.'

Shem looked relieved and even smiled slightly. Alissa remained stony-faced.

'What I also know is that you allowed yourself to be duped by this man and that brings into question your ability to carry out your duties. I'll report back to Garret the information you have given me today and a decision will be made as to your fate on board the Ark. Continue your duties as normal and I will contact you when that decision has been reached.'

Shem shook his head as Alissa rose to her feet. He reached out and grabbed her wrist.

'Please, Alissa. You can't do this.'

'I have to.'

'No, you don't. You're doing this to avoid talking about what happened with us.'

'This is not about our personal relationship, Shem. You messed up here and I have to do what's right for the safety of this ship, its crew and passengers.' Alissa's voice was gentler now. Seeing Shem so upset was killing her, but she had a job to do. Garret didn't hire her to play favourites with her friends. Shem had made a bad choice and he would have to face the consequences.

'Alissa, please. Think about this.'

'Let go of my arm, Shem.'

Shem's grip loosened, and Alissa turned from him and walked out of the room. As the door slid closed behind her, tears welled up in her eyes. She headed back to her office to write up a report for Garret.

CHAPTER SIX

'SO, WHAT DO YOU THINK?' CLARK LOOKED expectantly at Megan, a smile spreading across his face. It was an infectious smile that caused Megan to follow suit. She found it impossible not to join in when the captain was happy. A thousand thoughts ran through her mind as she looked at him, ring in hand, down on one knee.

'Is it too soon?' she said. 'Maybe it's too soon.'

'Megan Harper, I know the history and character of every woman in my crew and I know, without a shadow of a doubt, that you are the only one I want to spend my life with. If I died tomorrow, I'd die happy knowing you felt the same way. So, one more time ...Will you, Megan Harper, be my wife?'

He was right. They would undoubtedly be spending the rest of their lives on this ship and Megan had found herself falling in love with the handsome man before her. This ship was designed for raising families – their lives would be idyllic.

'Okay.'

'Okay? Just okay?' The captain had barely dared to hope that this perfect woman would marry him.

'Okay as in yes. I would love to be your wife.'

Clarke leapt to his feet and wrapped his arms around his new fiancé's waist, lifting her off her feet and holding her tightly to his chest. Megan squealed involuntarily. Once her feet were firmly back on the plush carpet, Clarke slipped the ring he had been holding onto her finger and smiled.

'Here's to us, and a long and happy life on board the Ark.'

Whilst it wasn't the proposal Megan had dreamed of, it was special and private, and that matched their relationship. No one really knew the extent of their friendship or how deep their feelings ran. Living and working together, things had developed quickly and in the few short weeks that they had been together Megan had found herself ever deeper in love.

She sank into his kiss. She knew that for the rest of her life she would never feel the caress of any other man, and she wouldn't want to either. This man would provide for her the life she had always dreamed of. Safe and loved on this ship filled with friends, joy and love.

Megan smiled as Clarke gently pulled her towards the bedroom.

***

'Look, can you fix it or not?'

The nav officer's voice was aggressive and it made Ham uncomfortable. Why was he yelling at him – he'd barely even started? The panel he was working on seemed to be all over the place. It was trying to perform actions it wasn't designed for. A faulty memory port, perhaps – sometimes they were cannibalised from other areas and this one could be trying to complete tasks it was originally designed for.

'I need to run a couple of diagnostic tests.' Ham tried to sound confident.

'How are you gonna diagnose anything? You're an idiot. How the hell did you pass the test anyway?'

The words stung Ham. Worse, if this man didn't know he'd cheated he would figure it out soon enough. They all would. Ham's fingers delicately removed the memory port and he stood up.

'I'll get this fixed. Please use another terminal until then.'

With that Ham turned and shuffled out of the control room. The vague feeling of guilt weighed heavily on him and he slumped off towards the engine rooms. With all the quiet space in there he could find somewhere to fix the port.

***

Arriving back at her office after her conversation with Shem, Alissa felt empty. How could she do this to him? Telling Garret the truth – that Shem wasn't experienced enough in the ways of human nature – would guarantee Shem a demotion that he didn't really deserve. He had only made one mistake. But that mistake could turn out to be a dangerous one, and Alissa could end up carrying the can for anything Stadler did while on board.

In her current state of mind the office felt oppressive, and when sat in her chair she sighed deeply, as though she could force all her stress out of her lungs if only she tried hard enough. The seat held her comfortably as she stared at the blank monitor on her desk, trying to make sense of her whole relationship with Shem, from finding him at her door for the first time to seeing him chained to the wall by Silver Glove. Her eyes felt heavy, and eventually she allowed them to close and rested her head on her desk.

The smooth sound of her office door sliding open made Alissa jump, landing perfectly poised to defend herself from the intruder. Seeing his face, however, drained her strength as it always had. He crossed the room, taking her hand in his own silver grip. Standing impossibly close to her, Alissa breathed in his presence and almost fell to the ground as her knees weakened beneath her.

'How ... how did you get here?' Her voice quivered with fear as she looked into his eyes. Such beautiful eyes, but all the rage was gone from them. Where there used to be anger and strength there was now only fear. He was barely recognisable as the man who had stabbed her in the belly.

'I need you, Alissa.' Even his voice was different, more strained. 'I need you to help me.'

'I can't.' The words came out as a kind of squeak as his hand touched her cheek. Alissa felt her stomach flip as his fingertips traced her lips, his eyes searching her face. With all of her might she hoped he would lean in; she held her breath, afraid that the slightest movement would cause him to lose his newfound humanity. The space between them began to disappear as he drew closer to her, his gloved hand snaking around her waist, pulling her in. This would be it. He was going to kiss her.

The crash brought her bolt upright in her seat, and her bleary eyes opened to reveal an empty office. Looking around for Silver Glove, Alissa realised she had dreamed him again. Her heart was pounding in her chest as she stood up and crossed the room to the door. Opening it, she found that one of her men had fallen off his chair, presumably asleep, and toppled over the metal table beside him.

Raising her eyebrows, Alissa smiled at the fallen guard.

'Get this cleaned up,' she said.

With that she left the security office and headed back to her quarters to sleep in an actual bed.

CHAPTER SEVEN

ALISSA WALKED INTO THE DOCTOR'S OFFICE   feeling exhausted. In an effort to sleep she had curled herself into a little ball under her covers and had gotten impossibly comfortable. But every time she closed her eyes she saw Silver Glove. The sleep she craved was broken by dreams of him, loving her and killing her. In the end Alissa had given up completely and had tried to shower away all thoughts of the evil weighing on her mind.

When Dr Harper arrived, Alissa was waiting for her.

'You look tired.'

'I need your help.'

As soon as the words left her mouth, Alissa remembered Silver Glove speaking them to her in her dreams.

'Having trouble getting to sleep?' Megan wore a little frown of concern. She had always thought Alissa young for a position of such massive responsibility.

'Getting to sleep is the easy part. It's the dreams that are the problem.' She regretted the words when the doctor raised her eyebrows.

'What dreams?'

Alissa looked at her hands, twisting her fingers around each other to avoid the doctor's eyes.

'I don't really want to talk about it.'

'Listen, if the dreams are causing the problem then that's what I need to fix. It may be a psychological issue rather than a physical one.'

Alissa looked up. She had worried that she might be going crazy but she certainly didn't want it confirmed. When Megan rested a hand on her shoulder, tears sprang into her eyes.

'I don't want to be crazy.'

Such a quiet voice, so afraid of the consequences. 'You went through a great trauma, Alissa. That would have an impact on anybody's wellbeing. Please don't try to force yourself into being strong, it won't help. Talk to me, tell me about the dreams, and be open, honest. You're safe in here.'

Alissa looked at the doctor's face, full of concern and kindness. 'I've been dreaming about him.'

'Him?'

Alissa looked back at her hands. 'Silver Glove.' It was almost a whisper.

'Okay, tell me about the dreams. What happens in them?'

'He appears to me. Sometimes we're on the ship and other times … It happens in different places – the Complex, the Facility, sometimes in places I've never seen before.'

'And what happens when you see him?'

'Sometimes he's hurting me.' Alissa was embarrassed to even say the words. 'Sometimes … he kisses me.'

She wished she could take them back as soon as the words passed her lips. Megan's eyes widened. Clearly the confession was shocking, Alissa knew it would be. The man had slid a knife into her and now she was having sex dreams about him.

'Alissa, he held you captive for a long time, I know that. And he did terrible things to you, took advantage of your trust. This is your subconscious' way of dealing with the emotions he's left you with. I have some old medical journals from many years before The Incident. They described a condition in which a captive forms positive feelings towards a captor. I think you may be suffering from something similar.'

Alissa looked at the doctor hopefully. 'So, there's something medically wrong with me? What's the cure? Can I take it now?'

'I'm afraid not. The treatment for such cases was intensive therapy to help you explore your feelings and separate the positive feelings from the negative influence.'

'So, the dreams won't just go away?'

'Not at first, no. But I'll help you. With time, patience and a good support network you can overcome this.'

Alissa allowed her eyes to well up, and she felt the doctor's hand touch her own. It was reassuring – at this moment, she needed the friendship above all else. Looking down, she noticed the ring on Megan's finger. Alissa grabbed her hand and looked at it.

'This is beautiful, are you engaged?'

The secret was out. 'Actually, yes. Yesterday.'

'To the captain?' Alissa asked the question tentatively. Nothing had ever been confirmed about their relationship but the rumours were everywhere. The doctor blushed.

'Congratulations.' Alissa smiled as she reached out and hugged her friend. The captain was a good man and he deserved someone as perfect as Megan. At that moment Alissa wished she was closer to the doctor, a better friend. She wanted to share in her happiness, to be a part, when the time came, of the blushing bride's wedding celebrations.

Alissa left the infirmary with her head reeling. Lives were truly being lived on this ship and here she was, focusing on a nightmare from the past. One that couldn't hurt her anymore. Silver Glove was gone and maybe they'd never find out where; it was time to live her life.

She craved her old life, and she was ready to work hard to get it back. The dreams would fade in time but Ham and Shem, all the important things – they would be there forever. With a smile on her face, Alissa headed towards the engineering section of the vast ship. Her heart was set on just being with Ham today, seeing his bright face.

On the other side of the large double doors that separated the engine room from the rest of the ship, carpeted floors gave way to metal grating and the walls were a patchwork of riveted steel panels. It was assumed no one would visit this area and luxuries had been kept to a minimum.

Ham had a workstation close to the engines. No one else had wanted it since the noise was deafening, but Ham enjoyed it. He found it therapeutic – the noise helped him to focus. When Alissa arrived, he was hard at work on the faulty panel. All its parts were brand new and there was no reason for a malfunction. If the hardware was sound, there must be an issue with the software.

'Hey whatcha doing?' Alissa's voice was friendly, albeit almost drowned out by the roar of the massive thrusters. Ham glanced up and his face broke into a smile.

'Oh, hey Alissa! I'm just looking at this.' Ham half-heartedly lifted the memory port at one end to show his friend, before dropping it back down again and hurrying over to hug her. As he reached her side he remembered Alissa's no-hugging-on-duty rule and paused awkwardly before wrapping her in his big arms. The guilt she felt was awful. Here was her best friend feeling unsure because of her silly rules. Good spirits and affectionate instincts getting the better of her, she threw her arms around Ham and hugged him tightly.

'I wanted to hang out with you for a while. Is that okay?'

Ham released her and nodded enthusiastically. 'Like before? At home?'

'Yeah, just like before.'

She smiled as she sat on a chair beside his desk and put her feet up in front of her, resting her heels on the edge and wrapping her arms around her knees. Ham looked back at the memory port. Technologically sound, he thought absently, before moving it aside to concentrate on the rest of his work.

They sat for hours and talked, Ham occasionally looking up from his work when he got overly excited about what he was saying and Alissa laughing hard at their inane chatter. It felt like the old days, and Alissa marvelled, not for the first time, at how so much had changed in just a few months.

'So, we gonna see Shem tonight?'

Alissa looked at her friend, her smile faltering for the first time. Shem was the last person she wanted to see after everything that had happened, but maybe a good talk about their night out together would clear the air and allow them to go back to being friends. She was feeling brave as she nodded.

CHAPTER EIGHT

LOOKING AT HIS FINGERS, ALL KNOTTED TOGETHER and knuckles white, Shem's mind wandered to the conversation he had had with Alissa. His job was at risk. He'd made a stupid decision and now he was going to have to pay for it. And the worst part was that it would be Alissa, the girl he loved, who would be ruining his career.

He shook his head and pressed the heels of his hands into his eyes. Time passed and he stayed in that position, going over their last conversation again and again. When the door chimed he considered ignoring it; then he realised it might be Alissa and he was across the room in a matter of seconds, frantically keying the panel beside the door to let her in.

What confronted him instead was a dishevelled and exhausted-looking Vincent. The man was clearly not well. His weight seemed to have plummeted since coming on board and Shem's nostrils told him the greasy creature probably hadn't bathed since either. Wrinkling his nose, Shem stood aside and let him in.

Vincent seemed hollow, almost deflated as he dropped onto one of Shem's chairs, his red eyes staring straight ahead.

'Vincent.'

No response.

'Vincent! Can you hear me?'

Shem was growing concerned. He'd heard of some pretty vicious space diseases and could feel his palms getting sweatier as he thought of the hundreds of ways a virus could kill him.

'Vincent ...' Shem crouched in front of Vincent and tried again. 'Can you look at me?'

Slowly the greasy head turned slightly and Vincent's eyes met with Shem's. His lips looked dry and Shem was about to get him a glass of water when he spoke for the first time.

'I can't do this by myself.' The words were barely more than a whisper.

'Do what?' There was no task assigned on board the ship that could cause this reaction in a man. Shem was growing more concerned by the second. 'Listen, I'm calling the infirmary, they need to take a look at you.'

As Shem turned to stand up he felt a vice-like grip on his wrist. Vincent was holding onto him with all his strength.

'I'm going to destroy this ship. No one will stop me!' He spat the words out and laughed as he let go. Shem backed away, hitting the wall before fully taking in what he'd heard. Spinning around, he pressed the emergency button on N.O.A.H's interface and a high-pitched alarm sounded to let him know that medics were on their way.

Vincent was still laughing as two burley men arrived, lifted him onto a stretcher and carried him out of the room. Shem followed them out. Since Stadler didn't have anyone else on board, he wanted to make sure nothing bad would happen to him.

Once in the infirmary, a nurse that Shem had never spoken to came over to look at Stadler. He watched as she passed instruments over his body and rows of data appeared on a screen behind his bed. Occasionally her brow furrowed; other times she nodded to herself. Vincent seemed to be dropping in and out of consciousness and Shem was genuinely concerned.

'Okay. Severe dehydration and sleep deprivation. Has he been turning up for shifts?' The nurse looked at Shem, who shook his head.

'He called in, said he was sick.'

'Okay.' The nurse noted it down. 'Did you or he alert medical?'

'I didn't, I don't know if he did.'

'Right.' She stretched the word, like she didn't understand, or perhaps believe, him.

'Did you at least do a visitation?'

At this point Shem was starting to feel queasy. 'No. No, I didn't.'

'Isn't he on your crew, Chief?'

The question, as innocent as it sounded, hit Shem hard. Yes, Stadler was on his team but he was one man in a group of twenty and Shem had been distracted as of late. But overlooking a crew member's safety was a concern and Shem's ability to do his job would be brought into question by more people than just Alissa.

'If you'll excuse me ...' Shem turned and left the infirmary. It was clear he wasn't cut out for his position,

60

which begged the question: Why on Earth had they promoted him?

Turning a corner, Shem walked straight into the captain. He stood to attention, showing Clarke the respect he deserved.

'At ease, officer.' A gentle smile spread across Clarke's lips as he looked at the nav chief standing before him. Such a young kid, with all the responsibilities of a man. Life wouldn't be fair to him – it hadn't been so far. He'd live out the rest of his life on this ship, might never start a family or have even a fraction of the joy a human should have in one lifetime.

Shem was thinking of all the things he should be telling the captain. About Stadler, the illness and his delirious threat to destroy the ship. But in doing so he would seal his own fate, probably get demoted to cleaning crew. It was a humiliation he just couldn't face.

The two men nodded at one another and continued in opposite directions. As he followed the route back to his quarters Shem began thinking about what Vincent had said. I'm going to destroy this ship, no one will stop me. Was it true? He looked just about crazy enough to actually do it. Sure, he might not be the best guy in the world; but destroying the ship? Even Vincent Stadler, insurance salesman, wasn't capable of that.

***

The following evening, Alissa wrote her report for Garret. She kept it basic. The explanation of how Stadler came to be on board stuck entirely to the facts of the situation and how Shem had followed the usual protocol in an unusual circumstance – hence the problems. At the end of the report she made a point of saying that as the

Jeni Swift | The Prison

chief of security, she would take personal responsibility for Vincent Stadler's actions on board the ship. A couple of keystrokes later and the report had vanished into the ether to appear on Garret's monitor across the ship.

Leaning back in her chair, she felt better about everything. That afternoon, after leaving Ham to his work, Alissa had headed over to see Shem. The whole visit had started quite awkwardly and Alissa had the urge to run again, but she decided to see it through. For whatever reason, Shem didn't bring up their encounter after the club and it was a relief not to have to discuss it at all. Instead, they caught up on each other's lives. Shem told Alissa about Stadler's breakdown and how he ended up in the infirmary, and Alissa talked about her catch-up with Ham and her decision to stop dwelling on the bad things, to try and focus on the good.

There was the underlying concern about Vincent, but Alissa brushed it aside since she finally felt like she was getting her friend back, and they spent a few special hours together before heading out to find Ham. It was going to be a good night at the Rec.

***

The weeks following were long and mundane. Garret was satisfied with Alissa's report and she returned to her regular duties, sorting out disputes between passengers, making sure her security teams were performing as they should and patrolling the many decks and corridors of the ship.

In the Nav Room, Shem's men applied themselves to establishing the ship's optimum route and Shen himself had regular meetings with the other nav chiefs to arrive at a consensus they could present to the captain.

62

Ham replaced the entire memory port with a new one and tossed the old one in his box of spares. The parts would come in handy for something, they always did. There were other minor issues throughout the ship but nothing that unduly concerned him. Perhaps if he'd been taking the enhancers he would've put the pieces of the puzzle together a little quicker.

Clarke and Megan made their engagement announcement to the ship. Their wedding would be a small affair, but all crew and civilians could watch it on their vid-screens. There would be celebrations in all departments. It would be a joyous day.

Vincent Stadler's release from the infirmary was relatively uneventful. The nurse had given him fluids and he had slept through two full days thanks to Dr Harper and her sleeping drugs. Although physically rested, he was plagued in his dreams by the General; even now, back in his own quarters, she was always watching him. He knew that now. One wrong move and she'd find him.

He had been testing the program on which he had worked so hard. It localised to whatever machinery it was installed into, then spread to every connected piece of software. He'd been careful to map out the test areas so as not to draw attention to his little creation, but the time had arrived. The plan was to install it in the engine room directly into one of the ships power couplets, from where it would flow directly to the engines. At the same time, the virus would spread throughout Engineering causing the entire rear section of the ship to malfunction – more than likely to explode. The promise made by the General was that she would be waiting for him outside one of the airlocks to take him to safety. He would have less than three minutes to get across the ship to her, but it would be long enough.

On his latest dry run, the engine crew must've thought him crazy, dashing from their offices, down the hallway and out of sight, only to return ten minutes later, out of breath and pink in the face. He explained it as his feeble attempt to get in shape, said the route was an easy one. Questioned about the ships many fitness centres, he mumbled about not liking the machines and wandered off.

CHAPTER NINE

THE TIME FOR ACTION HAD ARRIVED. IT HAD BEEN a week since Vincent had been released from the infirmary and he was ready. Upon awaking he showered, shaved and dressed in his cleanest uniform. He must look as presentable as possible when he met the General for the first time. It was difficult to control the butterflies going wild in his stomach, and a strong cup of coffee only made it worse.

Finally, excited for the day ahead, Vincent headed to the Nav Room for his last day on shift. When he arrived at his desk he found Shem clearing away his things. First he felt confusion, then anger. How dare they touch his stuff?

'What are you doing, Mitchell?'

Without looking up Shem said, 'Clearing your work-station. It has come to light that you were less than honest in your attempts to board this ship. You manipulated me and numerous other people in your desperation to get on the manifest. As a result, you've been stripped of your rank and will now be added to the cleaning rota.'

Vincent felt the rage bubbling up inside him. 'After today,' he said, 'it won't matter! You'll be wishing you'd been a little more forgiving.'

With that he stormed out of the room, his words ringing in Shem's ears, viciously spat out like the words he spoke in his delirium. I'm going to destroy this ship. No one will stop me.

Shem's mind raced back to the night Vincent gunned down an Unpleasant One back on Earth, and his look of pride at doing so. It was the moment Shem had realised he had no idea what Stadler was truly capable of.

Alissa had submitted her report, and the captain and Garret had had a long discussion about the best course of action. The weasel-faced man had seemed more like an annoyance than a threat, so it had been decided that he could avoid a prison sentence by working the cleaning rota.

When the captain relayed this to Shem, he spent a considerable amount of time talking Shem through the processes he should be following. Clarke had the greatest sympathy for the kid who had made a wrong decision – after all, he'd made a few himself. Before Shem left the office, the captain had asked that he contact him directly if Stadler made life difficult for him. It was no secret that Clarke was looking for any reason to come face to face with Stadler again, and to make him feel the same fear he had felt when he chased Clarke and his son down a corridor back on Earth.

Shem decided to tell the captain about Vincent's re-action to his demotion, and also to confess what he hadn't told another soul. Ordinarily he would be speaking to Alissa, as she was security chief and responsible for anything that might compromise the safety of the ship; but the captain had been explicit in his instructions. He keyed in Clarke's comms ID on the communicator, and the captain's popped up on the screen.

'Captain, I'm concerned about something Vincent Stadler said. I think the ship may be in danger.'

Clarke furrowed his brow, making him look older than his years.

'What's been said?'

'Sir, a week ago, in a state of delirium, he told me he was planning on destroying the ship. I've just seen him now and' – he paused, trying to find the words – 'I think it's going to be today. We have to stop him.'

'Follow him. I'll keep your location tracked. I'm going to alert security and meet you as soon as I can. Don't let him out of your sight.'

'Understood, sir.'

Shem killed the communicator, turned away from the desk and headed out the door in the same direction as Stadler.

***

Captain Andover turned off his monitor and rubbed his face hard with the palms of his hands. Then he pressed a few keys and Alissa's face appeared. Her voice seemed to fill the room.

'Captain, how can I help?'

'The ship may be in danger. Vincent Stadler is involved. Shem Mitchell is following him to keep eyes on his location. Please monitor – and log their position as soon as you can.'

Alissa's face darkened.

'Yes, sir.'

She disconnected and asked the computer to bring up Shem's location. All senior members of staff were tracked in this way by N.O.A.H so they could be located in an emergency. She pressed some more keys and opened a channel providing direct communication with all on-duty security officers. They had drilled in the strategy to trap a dangerous individual many times, but had never needed to use it.

'All stations. Operation mousetrap is currently in effect on crew member Vincent Stadler. He is being tracked by Shem Mitchell – please use him to organise your movements. Be aware, Stadler is an unknown and may be dangerous. This is not a kill mission but do not hesitate if innocent life is in immediate jeopardy.'

As the words left her lips it occurred to her how she had become detached enough to issue a kill command – albeit conditional – without hesitation to a group of men and women she had barely taken the time to know.

Pushing aside the thought, Alissa walked out the door, aiming for Shem's location.

***

Stadler heard the footsteps not too far behind and cursed his own anger. He shouldn't have lost it on the nav deck but Shem had really gotten to him.

The mini terminal he held in his hand had its uses. He keyed in his position and it showed all the officers with similar devices in the vicinity. Mitchell wasn't too far behind so Stadler stopped in his tracks. Shem also stopped. Neither moved for a minute. Stadler didn't take his eyes of the little screen, not daring to look behind for fear of provoking Shem. He doubted the nav officer would be brave enough to tackle him all by himself, but he might alert someone else. Stadler walked on, slightly faster than before. He waited until he had turned a corner and was out of sight before breaking into a run towards Engineering. He could get there in less than a minute if he had to.

Shem turned the corner but all he saw was an empty corridor. Swearing under his breath he started running, hoping he was still heading in the right direction.

Captain Andover had followed Shem's movements, and it was clear to him that he was heading to Engineering – a good place from which to attack the ship. When the little marker that represented the nav officer suddenly started speeding down corridors, the captain realised that Stadler must have slipped away. He watched as the marker hit an intersection in the corridor and hesitated before speeding to the left, away from Engineering and towards the civilian centre. Clarke leapt to his feet and out the door. To cover all bases, he would go to Engineering.

***

Stadler reached the door to the engine room and frantically hit at the panel until the door slid open. Rushing inside he pulled a disk out of his bag and ran to the terminals at the back of the room. He loaded a screen and began typing commands. A scrolling green line denoted the drive bay and he inserted the disk. Stadler had encrypted it case of his capture, so a further series of keystrokes were required before the terminal began processing the information within it. He worked fast, trying to load the programs and enter the passwords before anyone caught up with him.

***

Clarke took every corner he came to at a run. The double door that was the entrance to Engineering was open, something that was against regulations. As he ran in he glanced through the archway that led to the engine room, and saw Stadler at the back, hunched over the computer terminal. Panic rose within him as he charged at the weasel, ready to drag him away, kicking and screaming if necessary.

'Back away from the terminal!' His voice thundered throughout the steel chambers.

Stadler turned to face the captain, smiling a grim little smile that turned into a grimace as Clarke grabbed his shirt and yanked him away from the terminal.

'What the hell did you do?'

Clarke's was shaking with a rage he could barely contain. Stadler, however, was laughing. The screen behind him read EXECUTION SUCCESSFUL – the program had fully installed.

'What's the program, Stadler? Tell me what it does!'

Clarke shook the little man to try and force an answer out of him.

The words tumbled out of his mouth between chokes of laughter. 'I've destroyed your ship. My little digital friend will work its magic in the engines and the ship will ... explode.'

The colour drained from Clarke's face.

***

Alissa was jogging along a corridor, every few moments glancing at the screen in her hand. Shem had run in one direction, but she had caught the captain going

70

into Engineering. Since her men were following Shem, she would follow the captain. Still running, she sent a message to Shem to tell him where the captain was.

Thanks, came the reply. I can't believe I lost him.

The chief nav officer was angry at himself. He had already run back to where he last saw Stadler and was trying to guess where he might have gone when he got Alissa's message. He set off at a run for Engineering.

***

The crunch of Stadler's cheekbone breaking under the captain's fist was the most satisfying sound Clarke could have asked for in that moment. He tossed the shrieking man to the floor and turned his attention to the terminals before him, barely noticing when Stadler dragged himself to his feet and slunk across the Engineering deck to the archway that led out to the offices, then the main corridors. His face was a crumpled mess of blood and he could barely see, running blindly into Shem Mitchell in the corridor. His former boss grabbed him and spun him round.

'Let me go!' The words came out as a gurgle.

'Not a chance, Stadler.' Shem held onto him, waiting for Security or the captain to arrive. 'Your captain is running out of time, as are you.'

As he motioned towards Engineering, a shrill alarm rang out and Shem's eyes widened. He let go of Vincent and ran into Engineering. A million things went through his mind; could it be a bomb? Was he going to die? Would he ever see Alissa again? His lungs burned before he remembered to breathe. The alarm was the signal to evacuate and the engineering crew were running past him in the opposite direction. Shem urged them to move faster, ushering them out and away from the department.

Shem heard the clang and thud of a blast shield dropping into place, and ran towards the sound as the last of the crew escaped.

The blast shield itself was a hulking metal wall a metre thick, built to withstand a direct explosion in the engine room. Relief flooded every vein in Shem's body and stopped and stopped and leaned forwards with his hands on his knees, taking in great gulps of air. Whatever was about to happen, the ship would be safe. If that was Stadler's mission, he had failed.

***

As Alissa turned the corner to Engineering, Stadler came hurtling towards her, running way too fast to stop. They collided and both fell to the ground, a groan of pain coming from Stadler's lips as his already beaten frame took a harsh landing. Alissa leapt up and reached out to grab him but he managed to get to his feet and her fingers just missed. They both took off down the corridor, Stadler looking over his shoulder every few steps and Alissa with nothing but determination on her face.

***

Shem was leaning against the blast shield, waiting for Alissa to get back to him on her progress with Stadler, when his communicator buzzed. He pressed a button to acknowledge.

'Who's out there?' It was the captain's voice.

Shem frowned. 'Captain? It's Shem Mitchell.'

'Shem Mitchell. Not who I would've chosen to have my last conversation with, but you'll do.' The captain chuckled. 'Listen carefully, Mitchell. Stadler did this. He input a virus into the engine control module. It looks like it's designed to cause critical malfunctions through some kind of chain reaction, right across the ship. I've managed to keep it localised to the engine room for the moment.' There was a short silence. 'I don't know when, but the engines will blow. I tried, but I can't prevent it. The only good news is that N.O.A.H dropped the blast shields to protect the ship.'

'Open them, captain. Before it's too late. Open them.'

'I can't. There's no override. I did what I could to save the ship. No traces of the malware will exist anywhere else on the ship. You'll all be safe.'

Shem felt the first vibration run through the ship, making his teeth chatter. This was really happening.

'Captain! I don't know what to do.'

There was no response. Shem had no way of knowing what was happening on the other side of the shield, but his feet took the lead before his mind had caught up and he found himself charging out of there, hitting the alarms as he passed.

***

Back in Engineering, Clarke sat on a stool and looked calmly across the room at a row of terminals that were crackling and sending cascades of sparks to the floor.

He placed his hands on his lap and waited.

Megan. At least Megan will be safe.

***

Alissa felt the second tremor, and frowned. The first one had been little more than a mild vibration, but this one was much worse. Just then the alarm rang out, and N.O.A.H began to advise people of the safest decks on the ship for emergencies. The next quake knocked Alissa to the ground, and she saw Stadler fall just a few feet ahead of her. Then she heard it – an almighty crash, metal and plastic screeching and twisting. The ship felt like it disappeared from under her as it heaved from the explosion. All the power cut out and there was only silence and darkness.

When the emergency generators cut in, Alissa saw Stadler disappearing down the next corridor. When she got to the corner and looked down, there he was, standing in front of an airlock, looking through the glass at a cloud of twisted steel and debris that was gently floating by. Alissa could barely take in what she was seeing. The ship, or part of the ship, had exploded – that much was clear. But there was no explanation. How could something so catastrophic have happened?

Her communicator beeped and she yanked it from her belt.

'Yes?'

'It's me.'

Shem's voice. Relief flooded through her, knowing he was safe. But he sounded so distant.

'What's going on, Shem?'

'Stadler did it. He blew up the engines.'

Alissa stared daggers at the back of Vincent Stadler and slowly reached for her weapon. She would drag him to the brig and he would rot in there for the rest of his life.

'Alissa, the captain's dead.'

The communicator fell out of her hand and hit the floor with a thud. Stadler must have heard because as she got closer, he turned to face her, his back to the airlock door.

'The plan was to meet here,' he said. His voice was flat, his expression haunted, devastated. 'Why did you lie to me?'

Alissa didn't reply. She leaned in close to him and pressed the panel on the wall, opening the airlock. He wasn't ready, and practically fell in before the door slid shut behind him. Alissa became vaguely aware of the sound of Shem's voice, calling her from the communicator. She didn't take her eyes off Stadler. The pathetic weasel had soiled himself and was weeping, curled into a tight ball on the floor. She hesitated for a moment before beginning the sequence to open the external doors.

Then she turned and walked away, as Stadler silently screamed his last breath from behind the door.

CHAPTER TEN

IT HAD BEEN A LONG WEEK SINCE THE EXPLOSION. The ship was running on emergency power indefinitely, which meant they were crawling through space at a fraction of their optimum speed. The chances of them surviving through enough generations to make it to the New World were slimmer than ever and while the backup power they had would keep the life support systems running for many years to come, they were essentially floating in the endless sea of space with no hope of rescue.

The crisis, for what it was worth, had brought the community together, civilians and militia working side by side to repair the damage and make the Ark liveable once more.

Then came the investigation. It was led by Garrett, Alissa's mentor. Reliving the day, even if only through words, was heartbreaking. The thought had crossed her mind that she had finally become the murderer Silver Glove had manipulated her to be, and while once upon a time just thinking that would have made her cry, it seemed that now all the tears were gone.

Clarke Andover's funeral was a poignant affair, held a week after the explosion and a mere three days before his wedding should have been. All crew were invited to pay their respects and every one of them showed up. Ham, Shem and Alissa stood together in silence. The entire event was shared with civilians on vid-screens. It took place in the gardens, the most beautiful space on the ship, the gathering bathed in starlight from the towering wall of glass.

There were rows of chairs, but no casket. The three friends opted to stand at the back – senior crew were invited to sit but Alissa decided against it. Megan sat at the front, with red eyes and tear-streaked face. Her heartbreak was obvious for all the world to see and for one bitter moment Alissa wished she had killed Clarke long ago, back in New Amerland, before he ever met Dr Harper. She would've spared this poor woman so much pain. And the fact was, she was still a murderer. A cold and clinical killer.

Fresh tears fell as Megan stood to speak of the man she loved. To tell his tale to every person on the Ark. Her heartfelt words were beautiful, and Alissa even caught a tear falling from Shem's eye.

It was all too much for her. She slipped away from the crowd and slowly trudged back to her quarters, allowing the bitter tears to fall.

She lay on her bed staring at the ceiling. Beige. Bland. Everything was bland. Why had the colour drained from her world? Was this what life became when you destroyed another human? Nothing felt real anymore; the entire world had edges that blurred and she wished that something would change, that she could feel happy again, that she could close her eyes and not see Stadler's anguished face as he begged for mercy.

'It's alright, Alissa. I'm here.'

The smooth, calming voice of Silver Glove wrapped around her and made her whole body tingle. It was intoxicating, but more importantly it brought the blurred edges back into focus.

The mattress shifted as he sat on the end of the bed and Alissa sat up. Silver Glove looked weak. His suit was no longer clean and pressed, his hair had begun to grow longer and his eyes were tired and hollow. The most disturbing part was his hand. It was the hand of a man. It was made of flesh and bone; the silver glove had gone. He saw her looking and smiled grimly.

'Perhaps I'll explain everything to you one day, but not today. Today I need your help.'

'I can't help you, you're not real.'

He moved closer and reached out his hand, tracing a finger along her jawline. A shiver went through her at his touch and she meekly mumbled her protest as his face drew closer to her own.

Closing her eyes, she allowed herself to be intoxicated by him. He whispered in her ear,

'Please save me.'

When she opened her eyes, he was gone.

***

Three months after the explosion, life was returning to normal. Garret had been sworn in as captain of the Ark and had moved into the Clarke's old office. He had remained in his own residence, however, out of respect for his fallen superior.

Ham continued his work on repairs to the ship's engines. All mechanical and maintenance crew were on call to fix the behemoth and together they had managed to get her moving a little faster through space.

CHAPTER ELEVEN

'I'M SORRY.' THE WORDS DIDN'T REGISTER AT FIRST. They felt alien coming from his lips as they echoed round the room. They sat facing each other in a room that looked to Alissa like the one she had slept in at the Facility. Only now it was completely empty except for a table and the chairs on which they sat.

Alissa looked down and bit the inside of her cheek to stop herself from crying. She picked at the little splinters poking up from the table top and frowned, choosing her words carefully.

'Did you do this?' Her voice was shaking but she was doing it. She was speaking to Silver Glove in a civil manner – she would not allow the opportunity to pass. 'Did you kill Captain Andover?'

Now it was Silver Glove's turn to look away. Did she catch a flash of shame? If so, it was gone in an instant and he was back to his usual confident self.

'No, but I know who is responsible.'

'Who?'

'Alissa, I don't have time to tell you all the things I wish I could. All I can say to you is that they know you're here. And they will stop at nothing to destroy this ship.'

This was the velvety voice she remembered, but now it was mixed with fear. And there was something else new, something she found deeply disturbing. The silver hand was gone, replaced by flesh and bone.

'Who knows? Who wants to destroy us?'

'I don't know their race. They keep their secrets from the humans held here.' His shoulders sank. 'Please, help me.'

Alissa almost jumped out of bed as she woke, drenched in sweat. As always, Silver Glove had plagued her dreams, but this time it felt much more real; she felt more connected to him. There was none of the violence of her nightmares, just a man begging to be saved. She would need to speak to Garret about it all – if she had learned anything from Shem's situation it was that keeping secrets helped no one.

The clock light was a bright point in the room. *Three a.m. Great*. Climbing out of bed, she stretched the dream away and walked to the wet room for a hot shower.

***

Sleepless nights were the new reality for Megan. Lying on her side on the couch, she let silent tears roll across her face and onto the cushion. The double bed seemed too big without Clarke. A sob escaped her lips when she thought about how they used to lie close, listening to music. It was one of Clarke's favourite ways to spend an evening. Soft, slow classical melodies from the database. There had been occasions where Clarke would jump to his feet, taking her with him, and whirl her around the small bedroom. Clarke Andover wasn't the best dancer, but he loved her. Megan turned her face into the cushion and wept freely.

Hours passed as she lay there, remembering her fiancé and aching to have him back. Megan had always thought of herself as a strong woman, independent, well able to look after herself. What she never expected was to lose herself so completely in grief. Eating became a chore, showering was a luxury her misery could not afford. While everyone else got on with their lives, it seemed only right that she kept his memory alive by reliving every moment she could remember, over and over again.

As always, her body betrayed her eventually. Megan stood and ventured slowly to the bathroom, with a blanket round her shoulders for comfort. Sitting down, she wiped the tears away as best she could with her hands and took a few deep breaths. The little monitor on the wall beside the cistern made an unfamiliar beeping sound as she urinated. When she was finished, she looked over her shoulder and realised she had just been told by a toilet that she was pregnant.

An early morning jog to the infirmary was not something Megan was accustomed to. It took the breath from her and when she arrived she took a minute or two to get it back. A young nurse with long, straight, jet-black hair pulled back in a high ponytail, and beautiful brown doe eyes, spoke to her with a thick accent.

'Doctor, what are you doing here? You've been granted bereavement leave.'

Megan's eyes welled up. 'I have to run some tests, Sahline. Please, will you help me?'

Megan sat on a high stool while Sahline drew three vials of blood.

'Are you going to tell me why I'm running blood tests? What am I looking for?'

Even as she asked the question, Sahline regretted it. The doctor's face crumpled and fresh tears fell.

'I'm sorry, doctor. I shouldn't pry.'

Sahline took the vials across the room and sat at a table filled with sophisticated-looking equipment.

'It's okay, I'm just feeling a little tired ... I think I'm pregnant.'

The nurse nodded gently and smiled before wrapping Megan in a hug that surprised them both.

The two women spent the next hour running tests to determine all they could about Megan Harper's physical wellbeing.

'You're definitely pregnant, Megan.' Sahline looked at the doctor with a mix of affection and concern. It was no secret that Megan had struggled to keep it together these last few weeks. How would she cope with a baby on the way? 'I'm here if you need anything. In fact all the staff here will be available to you. You know that, right?'

Megan nodded and stood up. She thanked Sahline for her time and help, but now she needed to be alone.

As it turned out, people didn't need to worry about Megan Harper's ability to bounce back. Within hours of finding out about the baby, Megan was showered, dressed for work and in the medi-bay treating patients with confidence. She would have the nights. They would be hers to remember Clarke and grieve for him, but the baby came first now, and she would not allow anything to jeopardise its safety. Now was the time to take care of herself physically, because it wasn't her body anymore, it was home to the most important life in the world and she would do anything to protect it.

***

The thing that upset Ham the most as he sat at his workstation, surrounded by blackened and twisted computer components, was the familiarity of the software he was looking at. The construction crew had finally gotten the hull sealed and released the pressure in the engine room. The place was a mess, the walls completely black and bubbled, the steel flooring warped from the heat. It was a miracle the bulkheads had sealed the place as well as they had, but anything that wasn't bolted down had been blown out into the blackness of space and would likely never be seen again. Some circuitry survived and was gathered up by the engineers to be fully inspected. The pieces were passed out to a number of mechanics and technicians to be thoroughly checked and compared to technology already on board. The fear was that Stadler might have created bypasses that could release whatever malware it was back onto the ship's systems and finish the job he started.

While Ham's fingers sped over the keypad, his thoughts kept turning to Shem. The decision had been made by Garret to confine him to his quarters since the accident, and Ham missed him. He could no longer just call him to catch up or go to the Rec for drinks. There was a security detail outside his door so Ham couldn't even go to him and say hello. Ham had taken to keeping a small digital frame in his overalls, with an image of himself with Shem and Alissa, laughing together. But it wasn't the same as seeing Sham. He had been taught in childhood never to speak ill of the dead, but at that moment he despised Vincent Stadler for ripping their small group apart.

84

As he continued work on the circuits, it seemed to Ham that the program installed by Stadler was crude but effective. Being honest with himself, Ham knew that he didn't fully understand what he was looking at. Hardware was his strong suit – he could repair any piece of tech that was broken – but programs and complex coding were beyond him. There was, however, a feeling he couldn't shake. It sat firmly in his mind, prodding at him and making him feel sick. It was the feeling that some time, somewhere, he had seen this program before. He knew that he didn't need the enhancers but the temptation to take the shortcut was too great. Everything would become clear to him and he would finally understand the finer points of the scripts. Above all, he would know how to make sure the ship was safe.

***

Alissa was sitting across from Shem in his living space, staring him down while he looked at the floor. The lights in the room were too bright for Alissa. They reminded her of the Facility, but she ignored her discomfort. She was one of only two people allowed in this room; the other was the new captain. The plastic chair on which Alissa sat was uncomfortable to say the least, but she had other things on her mind and so here she sat, hoping that something would distract them from what was happening.

They had sat in silence for an hour now, Shem awkward and Alissa hard-faced, but he still couldn't bring himself to meet her gaze. The words to describe what had happened didn't come easily, and neither of them were willing to start such a difficult conversation.

Finally, Alissa took a deep breath and started what she feared might be the last talk they would ever have.

'Shem, our captain died.'

'I know.'

'Do you? Do you know the implications? You brought Stadler on board. You didn't check his credentials, you failed to notify me of threats he made against this ship and her crew, you knew the captain was suspicious and yet you failed to follow up when Stadler's work deteriorated. Shem, I can't protect you from this.'

For a few moments Alissa stared hard at Shem's face. He still couldn't look at her and finally she lost her temper. She stood with some force and Shem's eyes flicked momentarily upwards. Alissa crossed the room to the window, and looked out at the stars. Part of her needed a moment to calm down; another part didn't want to risk bursting into tears in front of Shem.

'Garret has decided to proceed with the court martial. Your trial is tomorrow at 14:00. No viewing will be permitted.' Her voice softened. 'He wants to keep this as quiet as possible, for your sake.'

Shem pursed his lips and rubbed his forehead with the fingers of one hand, as if blocking out an inner turmoil. She was right, of course. Everything that had happened here was his fault.

The disciplinary meeting with Garret hadn't gone well at all. The new captain had belittled and verbally bashed Shem for his naivety and stupidity. Shem sat in silence while every little thing he had done since he was promoted was scrutinised. Including his private life. Explaining Sophia while Alissa was there was the most uncomfortable and awkward thing he had had to do in a long time.

Now, he would be thrown into the brig for the rest of his life on this ship.

I wish Ham was here.

***

Ham was sat on his bed with a blood-spotted tissue pressed to his nose. His eyes were shut tightly and in his other hand was a small clear packet, empty.

One more look at the software – that's all Ham needed now and the whole thing would be resolved and hopefully, what was left of the ship would be saved.

Leaving his quarters, Ham looked along the deserted corridor. The ship had been quiet recently and he didn't like it. As he passed Shem's quarters the door slid open. He stopped for a moment, hoping to see his best friend. While he was surprised to see Alissa, it certainly wasn't a bad thing. Ham smiled warmly, went to give Alissa a peck on the cheek and changed his mind, greeting her with a handshake instead.

Alissa didn't return his smile. 'You're on the enhancers, aren't you!' she said. Anger from Shem's behaviour clearly hadn't subsided yet and here he was, on drugs. He hissed at her to shush.

'Without them I can't do my job. And if I miss something, more people might die, so just leave it. How is he, anyway?'

'Shem? He's coping for now.'

Ham frowned. When the drugs wore off his primary emotion would be distress, but for now he just felt concern.

The two friends parted ways a few corridors later and Ham arrived back at his workstation. He sat at one of the workbenches and cracked his knuckles.

'Okay, what secrets are you really hiding?'

87

As Ham switched the system back on and watched the lines of code flit past his eyes, he was distracted by thoughts of Shem. It would be a great shame if they became separated, but it would be even more difficult, he assumed, for Shem and Alissa.

Something about the software still perplexed him. He had seen this before, he knew he had. This was the virus from the damaged memory port, the one he had tossed aside when it didn't make sense.

Stupid, Ham.

In that moment he realised that all this could have been avoided if he had just been smarter.

CHAPTER TWELVE

'I AM CALLING TO ORDER THE TRIAL OF SHEM Mitchell. This is a closed trial, authorised attendees as follows: myself as acting captain, Alissa Namaah, chief of security, the defendant Shem Mitchell and his counsel Aiko Tanaka, and Carl Goodacre, prosecuting on behalf of the Ark and its inhabitants.'

Garret slammed a small wooden sphere onto the table firmly, then laid it on a little disc with an indentation to hold it in place.

'Please all sit.'

As directed, the room sat solemnly as the trail of Shem Mitchell began. It was being held in a section of the ship that few people ever saw. The room was empty but for three small tables set onto a slightly raised floor at one end, and twenty seats arranged in four rows. Garret sat at the centre table with a digital pad in his hand, reading the details of the case that been presented to him. Shem sat at the table on the left with Aiko, a pretty

Asian woman with a straight black fringe and the rest of her hair pinned up, while Carl, a slightly fat and rather unattractive man, sat with Alissa on the right.

Shem had to admit that the trial was being conducted very professionally, but he had never felt more alone – or more judged. Aiko had done the best job she could by way of preparation. She had taken the time to listen to everything Shem had to say and had worked hard to understand his position, ultimately agreeing that he wasn't responsible. The defence rested on shining a light on the fact that Shem had received no prior leadership training and had been left to his duties as normal. That Captain Andover had assumed he was prepared for a job he never really thought he would get. Aiko argued that Clarke Andover was just as responsible as Shem for the situation in which the nav officer found himself.

The prosecution, on the other hand, pointed to every decision Shem had made that lead to Stadler being on board and allowed to roam freely. Alissa was called as a witness. It was the worst moment of Shem's life when she detailed the conversation they'd had in which she warned Shem to watch Stadler – only for him to ignore her advice.

'Garret– I mean, Captain ...' Alissa said. 'Captain, you cannot hold Shem solely responsible for the incident that occurred. I made the decision to keep Stadler on board and I made the decision not to throw him in the brig.' She took a deep breath. 'As security chief on board the Ark it is my responsibility to keep the ship safe. I failed in my duties – not Shem. I should be on trial and I will accept any punishment that comes my way.'

His brow furrowed so deeply that Alissa swore his eyebrows became one.

'Alissa Namaah. You are not on trial. You've given your statement; now kindly take your seat and your actions will be addressed at a later date.'

Shem watched her as she sat back down. After trying to throw herself under the metaphorical bus for him, she still didn't even glance his way. His career was over, but hers didn't have to be. He would accept everything they threw at him and keep Alissa out of it.

As the trial continued, Shem started to zone out. Aiko and Carl were having a debate about officers' responsibilities. It was people he didn't know arguing over his future and he had no way of changing their minds. In due course he was afforded the opportunity to explain himself, to put forward his side. There were gasps when he quietly declined.

Alissa jumped to her feet. 'Shem! You have to tell them your side, tell them what happened.'

Shem slouched further into his chair and put his head in his hands.

In the end Garret sentenced Shem to twelve months in the brig – a reflection of how he viewed the severity of the offence. Aiko was pleased – the sentence they had been looking at was up to seventy years. Garret must have really believed in Shem's defence. Upon release, Shem would be added to the cleaning rota to ensure he spent the rest of his days on board working. He would never be permitted to enter the civilian centre.

The door opened and two of Alissa's men – burly, expressionless types – walked in to take Shem to the brig. It took great self-control not to burst into tears. How could they think they needed guards like this to escort a broken man? Deftly, she avoided Shem's gaze – and now it was up to her to tell Ham the result of the trial, to break the news that Shem would be locked away for a year.

When Alissa arrived at Engineering, Ham was hunched over his workstation, his head resting on his arms. He was snoring gently. She leaned against the door frame and watched him. For the most part the other mechanics left him to his own devices, but there was no respect for the bulky man who talked like a child. Rumours had circulated among the engineers about Ham's aptitude test – they said there was no way he could've passed it without help. Not many of them liked Ham. They thought he had taken the job of a man that could've been so much better.

Alissa didn't care about any of it. All she wanted was to protect Ham from the cruelties of this life. Smiling, she crossed the room and brushed her hand against his cheek.

'Ham, wake up.'

Her voice was soft and kind and Ham's eyes slowly opened and found her face.

'Oh, hey! How'd you get in my room?' He surveyed his surroundings, 'Oh, I'm still here.'

'How do you feel?'

'I'm okay, just tired now.'

'You need to stay away from the enhancers. They'll start to mess with your head.'

Ham didn't respond. Instead, he smiled and hugged Alissa. 'How was the trial?'

Her face was squashed into his meaty shoulder and she gently extracted herself from his embrace before she answered.

'That's what I came here to talk to you about.' She took his hands in her own and held them tightly as she continued. 'You know that Stadler was the one responsible for the attack on the ship right?'

Ham nodded.

'And you know that Shem was the one who gave him the job and brought him onto the ship, right?'

He nodded again, and his brow furrowed. He rose to his feet. 'Yeah, I know all this. Just tell me what they said.'

Alissa looked at the floor. 'He's in the brig. He'll be in for twelve months.'

Ham's eyes welled up and his bottom lip trembled. He began to quietly sob into his hand. Alissa wrapped her arms around his shaking shoulders and held him.

Alissa walked Ham back to his quarters and promised they would go and see Shem soon.

'No, Alissa.' Ham was standing in the doorway to his quarters. 'I don't know why, but you and Shem aren't right, just now.' Alissa looked down the corridor, as if checking to see if they were being watched. But it was more to hide her own discomfort. 'If you come with me to see him, it won't be like old times. It'll be something else, and I don't want that.'

'Ham, I'm a professional—'

'No. I'm going by myself, Alissa.'

He stepped into his quarters and the door closed behind him. A steel barrier between them. He knew it wasn't Alissa's fault this was happening, but he couldn't help but blame her.

It was around seven thirty in the evening. Ham cleaned himself up and changed into a shirt and pants that were clean of oil. Carefully he combed his hair and looked in the mirror. Satisfied that he was looking his best, Ham set off for the brig.

The transit system on the Ark was designed to travel vertically as well as horizontally to ensure that each part of the ship was quickly accessible. Ham pressed the button to call a pod and began his journey to see Shem.

***

Alissa lay down on her bed and for the first time since the funeral, allowed the tears to fall. This had been the hardest thing she had ever gone through, harder still for Shem. The idea of him down in the brig, alone in a cell, plagued her mind. She still cared so deeply for him – she might be disappointed in him, but she would never stop caring. Maybe she would tell him tomorrow. The last image in her mind, as she drifted into a deep sleep, was Shem.

***

The Ark's prison system was a lot more humane than the ones back on Earth, but it was in no way comfortable or pleasant. The main entrance was an unlabelled steel door with a fingerprint scanner. It would open from the outside for any crew member and it kept a log of every person in and out. Ham pressed his thumb against the soft plastic and the door slid open. A dark-skinned woman sat behind a semi-circular panel of monitors and controls, her fingers dancing as she typed, glancing at the screens every few moments. Ham approached her and smiled.

'Hello, please can I visit my friend?'

Without looking up she replied, 'Prisoner name?'

'Shem Mitchell.'

'Please proceed down the amber corridor to cell B17.'

94

There were three exit doors. A red one behind her, a green one on the wall to her left and an amber one on her right which was currently open. Smiling less now, Ham followed her pointing finger to the amber doorway. As he stepped through she pressed something on her panel and the door closed behind him. The corridor was brightly lit, allowing Ham to see into each box-like room through a clear door. The doors looked like plastic but had a shimmer to them that was different to anything Ham had seen. Walking along the corridor alone was an unsettling experience. Many of the cells were empty but some were occupied and Ham felt as though unseen eyes were following him. No matter how hard he tried to keep his eyes on the floor, he had no choice but to keep glancing up as he walked, checking off the cell numbers.

Finally he reached B17, and when he turned to face the doorway and look inside, it melted silently away to reveal an open archway. Shem was lying on his bed, facing the wall, completely unaware that he was no longer alone.

'Shem? Is that you?'

At the sound of Ham's voice, Shem turned and sat up on the bed. He stared for a few moments before leaping up and wrapping his arms around Ham.

'Hey Ham. How's it going?' They looked at each other for a long minute.

'I'm okay. Scared, though.'

Shem coughed slightly as Ham spoke, and touched the fingers of one hand to his forehead, shielding his watering eyes.

'I know man. Me too. But it's only a year, then I'm back out and we can hang out.'

'You promise?'

Shem put his arm back round Ham. 'Sure I do. I absolutely promise.'

***

The white-tiled walls were bright as she opened her eyes, and at first it was hard to focus. There was a burning sensation in her arms and shoulders and looking up, Alissa could see that she was chained to the ceiling by her hands.

The chains rattled as she struggled against them, the sharp steel shackles tearing into her skin and releasing little rivulets of red that ran down her bare forearms.

'HELP ME!'

Her voice was loud and echoed off the tiled walls. As she struggled, a silver hand reached round her waist and held her, lifting her slightly and taking the weight off her aching shoulders, while another unlocked the shackles. Alissa dropped slightly, and she turned to face her captor.

'Why am I here?' she said weakly.

'My love, my Alissa ...' He caressed her face. 'You have to come here. You have to save me.'

'Where are you?'

Silver Glove smiled.

CHAPTER THIRTEEN

'THIS ONE WAS MORE REAL, MEGAN. MY SHOULDERS actually ached afterwards.'

The doctor raised an eyebrow. 'What did he say to you?' She was keying everything into a wafer-thin tablet.

'The same as always. He said that he needed me to save him. That he was locked away somewhere and if I didn't help him, he would die.'

They were in Megan's private office. The doctor had decided that is was the best place to conduct this type of therapy. The last thing she wanted was people listening in to the chief of security's dreams about psychopaths begging for help. Multiple certificates from universities in Silver City adorned the walls, a number of which were for psychology and psychiatry.

'How do these dreams make you feel?' Megan knew it was a cliché, but it needed to be asked.

'I don't know. Scared, I guess. But also … happy, maybe? It's confusing. I know he's a monster, but …' –

she paused to choose her next words – 'it feels like he's my monster.'

'Your monster? Like you own him?'

'No. More like, he was made for me. Like everything about him was designed to appeal to me. So that I would trust him, let him torture me, so that I would do as he asked. That I'd be obedient.'

Megan stared at her notes for a while. 'This is all really good, Alissa. You're doing so well here. But there's something else I want to do.'

She rose from her chair and walked round the table to sit beside Alissa.

'I want to scan your brain.'

***

They arranged to do the scans after lunch to allow Alissa the opportunity to discuss it with Garret. It was quite an in-depth process and would take a few hours; it was only fair to keep him in the loop since he was captain now.

At the door to Garret's office, Alissa straightened her uniform as she waited for Garret to invite her in. When the door slid open she stepped inside. It was the same as always. You wouldn't know, she thought, that this man was the captain by looking at his workspace, but you'd know by the stress on his face.

Many times before, she had sat at the captain's desk for debriefings or assignments, but it felt different now.

'I'm glad you're here Alissa. I wanted to tell you I have assigned myself a first officer.'

Garret looked uncomfortable. It's about time, was all Alissa could think.

'Her name is Alice Underwood; she does prefer the use of her surname only so bear that in mind when you report to her.'

Silence fell as Alissa processed the words.

'I'm not reporting to you anymore?'

Garret shook his head. 'Not for the mundane, no. I am, unfortunately ...' He paused again. Old habits. '... too busy.'

Everything was changing around Alissa and it was becoming a bit much to take. Things that made her feel safe were slowly slipping out of her grasp. She tried to find words to explain but was interrupted in her thoughts.

'What can I do for you, Alissa?'

'I'm having a brain scan today. To see if I'm either insane or brain damaged from my Silver Glove experience. I hope that's okay?'

Garret's eyes closed while he took a moment. He was not a man to react emotionally and he would ensure his next words were chosen carefully.

'Who authorised the scan?'

'Doctor Harper.'

He nodded. 'Alright then. Let's invite her here to discuss the procedure in a little more detail.'

***

It was probably no more than half an hour since Alissa had left Megan's office and yet here was a message from Garret requesting her urgent attendance in his office. With a sigh, she put on her lab coat and walked out the door.

When she reached Garret's office, Alissa was sitting at the desk looking sheepish and Garret was pacing the back window slowly. They waited quietly for Garret to return unhurriedly to his seat.

'Doctor Harper, please can you explain to me why my security chief believes she may be brain damaged by the men in the Facility?'

Megan glanced over to Alissa then back to Garret. 'Sir, I diagnosed Alissa with Stockholm syndrome and have been conducting therapy sessions.'

Garret was nodding along as she spoke. She twisted her fingers together, took a deep breath and continued with her theory. 'Although many of her symptoms are typical of this syndrome, there are a few things that are bothering me.' Megan looked again at Alissa. 'You're very self-aware, Alissa, but there is something you said in our last session, about Silver Glove. You said he was made for you.'

For a moment the room was deathly silent. Garret looked confused, as did Alissa, and each of them tried to leap ahead of Megan's thought process.

'He was a hologram, that much is agreed by everyone. But I don't believe the hologram was from Earth; and I think someone – or something – did make him specifically for you, Alissa.' Again, she paused. It was difficult not to sound unhinged when people were staring at you while you talked about paranormal manifestations. 'I think there's still a physical connection. And I want to scan your brain to find it.'

The three sat there looking at each other. Eventually, Garret broke the silence. 'How quickly can we get this underway?'

***

Alissa was strapped into the scanner. If there was something in her brain, then they wanted to be prepared in case it tried to control her to protect itself. It felt like paranoia, but Alissa was insistent, saying it was for the safety of the crew. The padded table slowly began to move into the scanner tunnel.

Megan was controlling operations from a windowed side room, with Garret beside her. With infinite care she adjusted the position of the table until Alissa's mind was totally invaded by a thousand precision-focused particle beams. The doctor spoke into a microphone.

'Hey Al, how're you doing in there?'

'I don't really like it in here guys.'

'It's okay, it doesn't take that long,' Megan lied.

In truth the scans took around two hours. They took a variety of different types of images and data from the machine and Megan looked keen to get started.

'Good job today, Alissa.'

The doctor barely even looked at her as she spoke – she was already immersed in the data.

Garret put a hand on Alissa's shoulder and walked her out of the medi-bay.

'Time to get some rest, Alissa.'

She nodded and they parted ways.

CHAPTER FOURTEEN

THAT NIGHT, SILVER GLOVE ENTERED HER DREAMS again.

To Alissa, it was becoming more like an escape from the ship, from her life. Together they would visit beautiful places but he always had the expression of a man who was hiding something. Afraid to end the dreams, Alissa never brought it up – instead she enjoyed the sights and the gentle conversation. He asked about her family. What were her parents like? Did she have any siblings? How did she meet her friends? How was work going, and did she enjoy it?

In her heart, Alissa knew this wasn't the man from the Facility, the man who haunted her nightmares. This man was gentle and kind. At the end of his arm was a hand, made of flesh and bone.

Upon waking that morning, she wanted nothing more than to slip back into sleep and carry on walking along a purple-sanded beach by a beautiful green ocean. Silver Glove had held her hand. It was the first physical contact since she dreamed of being shackled in the Facility. It felt strange to her, but she allowed the feeling in, keen to see what happened next.

As it turned out, nothing happened. They had talked until she woke up.

It had been a couple of days since her brain scan and the day had come for her to go and see Shem. The last few times Ham had invited her to the prison sector, she had made up some pretty terrible excuses not to go. But underneath it all, she missed him desperately and wanted to talk to him.

It was this desire, added to the need to talk to someone about everything that was happening to her, that made her pluck up the courage. The first visit would be rough and there was a lot she wanted to tell him, without having to explain everything to Ham – the last thing she wanted was to scare her friend.

Her uniform would suffice for the trip; it would save her changing again to start her shift. She grabbed it from the floor, tossed it onto the bed and headed to the wet room for her morning shower.

***

The doors of the prison sector slid open and she walked to the front desk. Sitting there was one of her security officers, a dark-skinned woman who preferred to be called Bourne. Alissa smiled briefly and gave her a nod.

'I'm here to see Prisoner 00821.'

Alissa kept her voice as steady as she could, and Bourne repaid the effort by not making small talk. She flicked one of many switches on her desk. The door to the amber section slid open and Alissa went through, looking straight ahead as it closed behind her and locked in place. The corridor was as grim as the outer foyer in its colour scheme and Alissa focused her attention on the cell at the end. Muffled voices came from the cells she passed. A few drinks and a scuffle would see you spend the night in the green sector, but this corridor was reserved for longer sentences. In here were thieves, and hackers. The red sector was home to a violent offender who brutalised a woman within the first three days on board; Captain Andover had seen to it that he would spend the rest of his life in a cell.

At the end of the corridor, she peered into Shem's lonely cell. He was awake, leaning against the wall with his forehead resting on his hands. The protective field melted away and she stepped nervously into the cell and cleared her throat.

'I'm sorry it's taken me this long to come down here.'

Alissa meant it, too. Shem was her closest friend and before the aptitude test, she would've told him anything. But she was a liar now, she kept secrets, she murdered people and walked away without punishment. Shem looked up at her as she crossed the cell and sat beside him on the hard bunk.

Alissa tried to get her thoughts in order and in the silence Shem must have noticed her discomfort.

'Look, you don't have to be here if it's too much.'

His voice was tinged with sadness as he turned his face away.

'It's not that, Shem. I mean, it's not great in here but ...' What to say next? How to finish this thought? 'Well, I missed you, you idiot.'

That brought a slight smile to Shem's lips and the two of them relaxed a little, sitting on the bed, leaning their backs against the wall. Alissa looked around the cell, unable to look him in the eye.

'I'm really sorry, Shem. I should have done more to stop Stadler. I should be in one of these cells.' She looked down at her hands. 'I killed him.'

The arm that wrapped round her shoulder was warm and comforting and Alissa gladly leaned her head against Shem's chest.

'You're not a killer, Alissa. You took out a terrorist who attempted to destroy this ship.'

Shem was so supportive – no matter what she did he would never turn his back on her.

'Stop it,' she said gently. 'Stop being so nice about this whole thing.'

Shem chuckled. 'Never.'

They sat like that for a while, reminiscing and laughing. The closeness was a joy to Alissa, it was something she craved and no one was more surprised than her that Shem was the one to satisfy that craving. She allowed her mind to wander while her head rested on his shoulder, and she thought about what life would be like with Shem.

CHAPTER FIFTEEN

BEING PREGNANT MADE MEGAN A LOT MORE AWARE of her bad working habits, like her tendency to skip meals and work through the night. Which, in her defence, had mostly stopped now but when there was something as interesting as the scans in front of her, she couldn't resist staying up late to pour over them.

Alissa's results differed from standard brain scans. It was as if disparate parts of her brain were forced into action at the same time, which would be bad enough, but then the visual receptors had been damaged by repeated bombardment by something as yet unidentified. Megan took a deep breath and held it in. She was certain she was looking at evidence the Facility had done something vicious and permanent to Alissa. Slowly she exhaled as she flicked through the scans, until she reached one with a shadow. That was when she frowned.

***

The buzzing of the comms pad jolted Alissa and Shem as they sat next to each other. Taking it from her belt loop, Alissa pressed Receive and Megan's face appeared.

'What is it, doc?'

The doctor raised an eyebrow at the greeting and stared at Alissa through the screen for a moment.

'I need you to come to the infirmary and see me and Garret. I've got some results here that I need to discuss with you.'

'Okay, when?'

'Now, Alissa.' The gentle voice came from off-screen, but it was Garret. Alissa felt the blood drain from her face, switched off the comms pad and eased herself away from Shem.

'What's going on, Alissa?' His face was the picture of concern.

'I don't really have time to explain it all now, but I'll come back later and tell you everything. Okay?'

When she arrived at Megan's office, the digital display on the door said DO NOT DISTURB and there was a moment of hesitation before Alissa pressed the panel and walked in.

'You made it sound pretty urgent. Am I dying or something?' The question was asked with a morbid humour, but the faces of her colleagues made her heart sink. 'Oh my god, am I dying?'

'No Alissa, you're not dying.' Megan always talked with such kindness, and at that moment, Alissa appreciated it more than anything.

'Then what is it?'

Garret stepped forward and motioned for Alissa to sit down while he stood behind Megan's chair looking over the two of them.

'Doctor Harper has found something disturbing in the scans.'

Alissa looked between the two of them. 'Okay. Just tell me what it is. Don't leave me guessing.'

'When I looked through the images, I found a shadow in your occipital lobe.'

Alissa sat open-mouthed.

'After investigating further, I located a small piece of circuitry that was implanted sometime in the last twelve months.'

Garret stood forward, the time for a bedside manner gone. His chief of security was infected with alien tech and he wanted rid of it as quick as humanly possible. Having anything of that nature on board the Ark was endangering the lives of every single crew member.

'Alissa, we need to perform surgery to remove and inspect the device.' His voice had never sounded so calm – it could easily be mistaken for callousness – but the slight twitch in his eye was a clear sign to those that knew him well. This was hard for Garret. 'A representative from Engineering will be selected to perform diagnostics under high security.'

Alissa, who had sat quietly throughout, finally spoke. 'When?'

Megan stood up. 'I'm going to perform the surgery now, Alissa. I need you to come with me.'

108

CHAPTER SIXTEEN

ALISSA SAT IN A CHAIR LOOKING AT THE BED. IT seemed okay, a little flat and no duvet, just a thin sheet, but she supposed it wasn't designed for comfort. In all honestly, she was just trying to keep her mind off what has going to happen next. A vibrating whirr clicked in and Alissa felt cold plastic pressing against her neck and running up to her scalp. In the end Megan shaved around two inches of Alissa's hair from the back of her head, securing the rest in a grip, then motioned Alissa over to the bed and lay her down on her back.

***

Ham sat in the infirmary staring at the time on his personal comms. Alissa had been in with the doctor for hours now and he was really scared. She had called him as soon as she found out what was happening. She explained that the doctor wanted to operate on her brain and she would like him to be there when she woke up.

Ham had been on shift at the time and started to worry about what his supervisor would say; but a few words from Garret and he was being ushered out the door. As soon as the door closed behind him, Ham ran to the medi-bay as fast as he could. When he came bounding through the door, panting and sweating, Alissa smiled and opened her arms for a hug.

'Hey Ham, I'm so glad you're here.'

He blushed. 'It's okay, I wasn't too busy. Plus, you may need me for something.'

The nurses had sat him on one of the beds in an adjacent room with some water, and for the first hour or so he had worked on his comms, updating software as best he could, but it was hard when he wasn't looking at the actual circuitry. Eventually he gave up and just waited for news. For a while he thought about trying to get a message to Shem but by the time it got through Alissa could have woken up, walked down there and told him herself.

Next door, Alissa was staring at the ceiling. She felt a little queasy, not really ready for brain surgery but also, not okay about living with alien tech in her brain. Megan pressed two small metal cubes to Alissa's temples. A monitor beside the bed began bleeping along with Alissa's accelerated heartbeat.

'Okay, I'm going to administer an anaesthetic.'

An IV was slipped into the back of Alissa's hand and a nurse came over with a mask.

'Take in a few deep breaths, Alissa. Then count backwards from ten.'

She didn't remember any more, but it wasn't a dreamless sleep. Alissa found herself standing in her old cell in the Facility. But it was falling apart, like time had caught up with it. The whole place was slowly crumbling. On the floor was a tray upon which sat a strawberry. Rotten and filled with maggots.

She walked out of the cell and into the long corridor. Big chunks of ceiling and wall strewn on the floor made it a difficult walk, but she continued down, looking into rooms as she passed. There was a room filled with desks, broken and tossed aside. That's where he told me about Andover. Continuing on, she stopped beside another doorway and stepped in. It was the cell with the torture apparatus. The one with the electric spikes. But it was rusted, and the spikes turned to dust as she reached for them.

'I'm sorry.'

The voice came from behind her. She turned and found herself face to face with Silver Glove. Glancing down, she made a mental note of his hand – flesh and blood.

'I remember everything they did to you in here.'

Alissa turned back to the machine. 'You mean everything you did to me.'

'It's complicated.' He sighed.

Taking a step forward, he took her hand in his. 'I'm not quite him, Alissa. And he's not quite me. But we are two parts of the same being.'

'You saw everything they did to me.'

'Yes, and I couldn't prevent it. I had no strength then. But I do now.' Silver Glove took her by the shoulders and turned her to face him. 'I will fight every day to see you, Alissa. But I still need your help. I need you to come and save me. Otherwise, I'll die here.'

'Where are you?'

'Alpha-seven-fifteen-Delta-twelve-thirty-two.'   He paused for a moment. 'There's one more thing, Alissa, that I need you to know.'

'You have my full attention.'

Before Silver Glove could speak another word, he was gone. The world around her turned to darkness.

***

Megan emerged from the surgical unit and walked over to Ham.

'She'll be waking up soon. Everything was great and she's fine.'

Ham leapt to his feet and ran straight into the unit in time to see Alissa being wheeled into a recovery suite. He followed them in and looked around. It was the same room they had put her in when she was hurt by Silver Glove. Pulling a chair over, Ham settled down to wait by her bedside.

***

By the time Alissa woke up Ham, Garret and Megan were standing round her bed. Her first thought was that they all looked okay – no one seemed particularly upset, so she assumed all had gone well. Ham reached out and grabbed her hand, smiling with relief. Looking at him Alissa couldn't help but smile in return. He had spent hours here for her and didn't even know why.

Megan spoke, her voice brusque and professional.

'We removed the device. We don't know what it does and it's not like it's written on the side ... However, it is intact and seems to be functioning. How do you feel?'

Alissa responded with the coordinates. All she received back were blank stares.

'That's the location. Silver Glove told me. He needs rescuing.'

Megan glanced over at Garret, who was already in-putting the numbers into a comms pad.

Alissa wiggled her toes and moved her head from side to side. 'I feel okay. A little achy but nothing too bad.' She reached her free hand up to her shaven head and felt around for the wound, but it was completely smooth.

Megan smiled. 'Yes. I am just that good.'

For a few moments there was silence in the room. Alissa's fingers were still investigating the shaven patch of hair, Ham was smiling at her from beside her bed and the doctor was checking Alissa's vitals. All in all it would've been a pleasant interlude, if not for the dark cloud hanging over them.

'I have compiled a list of people from Engineering that I believe would be qualified to inspect the device,' Garret said. 'You've worked with a lot of these people in the past, Alissa, so please, take a look and tell me who you recommend.'

She took the comms pad and studied it, looking for Ham's name. It wasn't there. 'Well, you don't want Gaby, or Sim. They're too busy and just between us, they can't keep their mouths shut.' She furrowed her brown as she continued down the list. 'I would also say no to Beverley, Yon and Simon. Kieron too. Their work is mostly good but there is definitely something a bit strange about them.'

Another ten names were read out and excuses given by Alissa as to why each of them wouldn't be right for the job.

Garret sighed. 'Do you have someone in mind, Alissa?'

'Actually yes. I'd want Ham to do it.'

113

Garret raised an eyebrow and Ham looked taken aback. 'I don't know about that, Alissa,' he said. 'I don't know that kind of tech very well.' He was still holding her hand but now it was a much tighter grip.

'You listen to me, Ham. There is no one on this ship more qualified. You were the one that figured they were holograms and you were the one working on their projection unit for weeks. You can do this easily.'

Ham smiled. Alissa always knew just how to speak to him to make him feel like he was good enough to be here. He loved her for that.

***

The recovery for Alissa was no more than a few hours. Surgery on board a ship like the Ark was nothing major anymore. The physical trauma healed quickly; the real recovery was getting the sedatives out of your system. Alissa felt a lot less alert than usual. Garret gave her the rest of the day off to sleep it off and she spent much of that time trying to convince Ham to work on the device. Eventually, with great reluctance, he agreed.

With a few extra hours on her hands, Alissa decided that now would be a good time to talk to Shem about everything that was happening. It was unfair to leave him in the dark about such major events in her life. She got dressed and left the infirmary.

Over in the prison sector, the hug between them was a warm one, and Alissa let it last a few moments longer than she usually would. She had made a decision about Shem. She would see what happened in a year – after all, she wasn't going anywhere, and neither was he. It helped her fall back into comfortable habits with him, and she plonked herself onto the bench in his room and motioned for him to join her.

'I want to tell you the truth about everything. I don't want secrets anymore.' Alissa watched Shem's reaction, part relief and part worry.

'Okay, go ahead.'

With that the verbal floodgates opened and Alissa told Shem every last detail. It started with her failing the aptitude test and the fear that she would lose her friends, moving on to the kidnapping and what she went through in the Facility. It was easy to see Shem stiffen when she told him about the torture, when he really understood what Silver Glove had put her through. After that she described the plot between herself and Garret to kill Andover and how she even considered killing Louis, Andover's son, before they found out he was a hologram and in Silver Glove's service. The colour drained from Shem's face at that point. He had never considered, even for a moment, how far she would have gone to accomplish the mission she was given.

When she moved onto the dreams, Shem's demeanour changed and he looked progressively more tense with each word. Alissa held nothing back, explaining how Silver Glove appeared to her, what he did to her and how she let him. It didn't even seem like he was listening when Alissa went on to explain the Stockholm syndrome, the brain scans, the surgery, and the potential for alien life being behind all of this. When she had finished, she waited silently for Shem to speak. When he did it was through gritted teeth.

'You dream about him?'

Alissa frowned. 'Yes. But I just told you aliens have probably tampered with my brain. Get some perspective.'

'He knifed you and you dream about kissing him.' The hurt in his voice was starting to show and he was getting louder. 'He mentally and physically tortured you and you go around having sex dreams about him? What the hell is wrong with you?'

Leaping up to her feet she turned to face him. 'Shem Mitchell, I have been your best friend for years, how dare you judge me for something I can't control.'

'You're right,' he yelled back, 'you have been my best friend for years, and yet you'd rather fall in love with a psycho murderer who hung me from the ceiling by my arms! Or had you forgotten about that part?'

Alissa took a step back. 'Of course not, Shem. But I'm not doing this on purpose.'

'Well, I think it's clear how you truly feel, Alissa. You'd rather have this monster in your life than me. So get out and go and be with him.'

'Shem, don't do this.'

He turned away from her. 'Get out.'

The walk back to her quarters was slow, the tears threatening with every step. Once there, she slipped into bed for comfort, allowing the duvet to warm her. When she closed her eyes she expected the usual dreams but instead she dreamed of Shem.

CHAPTER SEVENTEEN

HAM SAT AT HIS WORKSTATION WITH A PACKET OF enhancement drugs in his hand. There was only one packet left – for emergencies only, he had told himself. So how had it come to this? Just when Alissa needed him the most he had barely any supply left. The attempts he had made at recreating the drug were miserable failures and had been one of the main drains on the resource he had left.

As he lifted the packet to his nostril, he closed his eyes and prepared for the burn.

It never got easier, no matter how much he used. It still felt like something was melting his nose and throat. As he threw the packet across the room to the bin a few drops of blood splattered onto the floor. He pressed a tissue to his nose until it stopped.

Within seconds his brain was working overtime, already thinking about the technology he had experienced back on Earth and how it could be utilised to create something so small. He opened the locked, steel box containing the small device. Leaning over it, he switched on a light and got to work. It was tiny, but it looked to be receiving data from something. Frowning, he pulled a monitor closer and worked on connecting the two.

Let's see what's going on in there.

***

Alissa felt numb. Like things had just stopped being real. It had been a week since the tracker had been removed and there hadn't been a single dream about Silver Glove. Far from the relief she expected, Alissa missed him. The visits had become a comfort to her, an escape from the life she was expected to live on this ship. Now all she could do was think about how different her life had become, with Shem not speaking to her and Ham taking enhancers again. She felt like she was alone. Even Megan had met some other mothers on board and was becoming good friends with them, leaving Alissa with nothing but her work to focus on.

So, she threw herself into her job, and the security team were not happy about it. Alissa worked them hard with drills and workouts. She became obsessed with ship safety, following her crew on their patrols and burying herself in training modules on the subject. It took one of the more experienced crewmen, Alistair Morgan, to talk her out of it. Alistair was the oldest man in the crew, with distinguished grey temples and green eyes that wrinkled sweetly when he smiled. He had worked security on ships for the last thirty-seven years and while his respect for superiors was unquestioned, his patience had started to wear thin.

Comms pads were strewn about her desk when Alistair arrived. He frowned as he walked in and she looked at him over her cup of coffee.

118

'Morgan. What can I do for you?' Even her voice sounded tired. *Probably from shouting drills.*

'I wanted to talk to you about your new approach to the team.' He perched himself on the corner of her desk.

'Yes, I'm feeling good about it. It'll get everyone in shape, and no one will ever threaten this ship again.'

Alistair sighed and rubbed his fingertips against his temples. 'You've been a great chief, Alissa. What happened isn't on you. But you're treating the team like they're the guilty ones. They work hard for you – you don't need to baby them or run them ragged or overwork them.'

For a moment there was quiet while Alissa digested his words. The team were the one thing she had left, and even they were tired of her.

'You're right.' She looked into her coffee cup, willing it to fill itself. 'Tell them you talked me round.'

When Alistair left, Alissa slouched down into her chair and closed her eyes, pressing her palms into the sockets. There she sat, alone, with no idea how to move on from all this.

***

The device had proven much more difficult to crack than Ham had initially thought. After the enhancers wore off on his first day trying, he had struggled. It was clear to him that the device was some sort of transmitter but he hadn't been able to figure out how to connect to it. He had known, of course, that it was imperative everyone knew what was being put into Alissa's brain.

That was when he had decided to use the last of his enhancers to clear his mind.

119

And now Garret, Alissa and Doctor Harper all sat in Garret's office looking at Ham. Alissa silently noted how confident and calm he looked, which to her meant he was on the drugs. It was a risky thing, standing in front of a doctor who knew him. The effects were undeniable. She looked around and could see that both Megan and Garret were shifting uncomfortably, avoiding looking directly at Ham. A blind eye would likely be turned if Ham was right on this, and silently she prayed he would be.

Ham stood beside a monitor and held the device out on the palm of his hand for them all to see.

'I have unpleasant news.' Ham surveyed his now captive audience and continued, 'The device is a tracking system and a transmitter. It uses the brain's REM sleep cycle to send data to the subject and receive their responses.' Ham paused for effect, and Alissa said:

'So everything I dreamed was planted in my head? I don't believe that.' Her voice was getting louder. 'Silver Glove was different – there's a real man out there, I know there is. One who needs us!' She was on her feet, facing Garret, and he stood up and said quietly:

'You are my chief of security. Sit down and pull yourself together.'

Alissa did as he commanded and sat quietly biting a nail. Garret sat down and turned his attention back to Ham.

'Please, continue.'

'I can't trace where the signals are coming from, but I can show you footage of the information that is being received.'

Ham pressed a couple of keys and the monitor flickered into life. There, before them, all was Silver Glove's smiling face. Over and over he was repeating coordinates in his silken voice, and Alissa sank into her chair. Megan, who had never seen him before, looked confused at first but quickly understood, from Alissa's reaction, who she was looking at on the screen.

'It seems,' said Ham, 'that this will play on a loop until interrupted by the receipt of information. Then someone at the other end will feed information dependent on that.' He turned to Alissa. 'This is designed to use you, Alissa. A receiver will have been installed in much the same way at the other end.'

Alissa's face contorted into a mixture of anger and horror. 'So there's another one? Implanted in someone else?'

Ham nodded. 'That's my assumption. I—'

'Who? Silver Glove? Aliens?' She whirled round to face Garret. 'What do we do? There were aliens in my brain.'

Garret stood. 'Thank you Ham, you're excused.' He nodded at the mechanic and Ham left the room, gently placing the tiny device on top of the monitor before he went.

When only the three of them remained, Garret picked up the little piece of alien technology, and stared at it, turning it over between thumb and fingers.

'We three have a decision to make regarding the co-ordinates we were given. But I feel that each of us is biased and cannot make a fair judgement that reflects only the imperative of the safety of this ship. For that reason, I'm bringing in Underwood. She has had nothing to do with any of this so far and I think she will provide us with a level-headed view of our predicament.'

Alissa and Megan nodded in unison. Alissa was desperate to save Silver Glove. He was out there and he needed Alissa to rescue him. Her decision was made:

whatever happened, she would fight with everything she had to save the man.

***

The meeting to decide the next actions of the Ark was not a short one. Alissa, Garret, Megan and Alice Underwood, Garret's second in command, all sat in a room with a vast table in the centre. Normally used for staff meetings and updates, it was considered neutral territory for such a critical decision.

'Taking the Ark into unknown territory, towards an unknown threat, could be a death sentence for each and every person on the ship ...'

Alissa listened carefully as Underwood presented her argument, and for the most part she had to agree that the second in command was right. Alissa wanted to take action to save a man who existed only in her dreams. Was it worth risking the lives of all on board?

When Underwood had finished, Garret turned to Alissa.

'Alissa, as chief of security, how do you feel we should proceed?'

'I ... uh ...' Her eyes darted around the room at each of the expectant faces. 'I want to save Silver Glove.'

Underwood raised an eyebrow and Garret sighed and made a little grimace. Everything had to be considered here.

When Megan cleared her throat, all eyes were on her.

'These life forms attempted to sabotage the Ark initiative to escape Earth by using Alissa to kill Clarke.' Even as she said the name, Megan touched her midsection and Alissa slid further down in her own chair. 'Then they used Vincent Stadler to try a second time to stop us.'

122

Garret was nodding as Megan continued. 'If we ignore them, if we just keep going our own way, they will try to stop us again. And who knows, maybe this time they'll succeed, and we will all die anyway.'

It was at this point that Garret rose to his feet.

'I should inform you that before we left Earth, the Government that currently resides on board this ship advised us that there would not be another Ark built after ours.' He paused to allow the new information to sink in.

'You mean that's it? Just us and those that went before us?' Underwood asked.

Garret didn't know Underwood well, but he knew her parents had left on the first Ark. This would not be an easy conversation.

'Alice, every Ark that has left our planet was destroyed, with no survivors.'

Underwood sunk back into her chair and Alissa watched her clench her jaw to stop the tears. Megan rested a gentle hand on her shoulder.

'These creatures have taken so much from us. We have all felt the pain of loss, some more than others. But if we don't go out there, if we don't face them, they will destroy us too.'

'And we might be the last of humanity.'

The three looked at Alissa when she spoke.

'I mean, if there's none before us, and none to follow … we will be the last surviving members of the human race. We have to live through this.'

'By the same token, if this ship does contain the last of us, then we cannot risk them taking or destroying it if we go after them.' Garret rested his head in his hands.

'What if the Ark didn't go?' Garret looked up at Alissa as she spoke. 'I mean, what if we get closer in the

123

ship, then send an away team on a micro-ship? There are dozens on board.'

'And who do you recommend I send on this potential suicide mission?' Garret was stern of mouth but soft of eyes. He knew her answer before she said it.

'Me. I'll go. I'll put together my team. People who know exactly what they're getting themselves into. We will find out why they want to destroy us.'

CHAPTER EIGHTEEN

GARRET SAT IN HIS OFFICE NURSING A GLASS OF whisky with one hand and rubbing his eyes with the thumb and forefinger of his other. Things hadn't gone to plan for him at all in this life. It felt like centuries ago that he had accepted the job of babysitting a ship on such a long journey that he would die of old age on board. If he was completely honest with himself, Garret expected to retire his commission within ten years and live out life as a civilian in relative luxury. Repayment for all his years of hard service. His long overdue reward. But now, Clarke was dead, Garret was captain and he had just ordered his crew to follow a set of alien coordinates in order to find out why they wanted to wipe out all of humanity.

And what of Alissa?

The girl was going to infiltrate a potentially hostile environment to rescue a man that may or may not exist. Had she not gone through enough? Was it fair of him to allow her to risk her life? Garret had never wanted to be captain, because a decision like this would weigh on him until the day he died.

He took another long drink and wheeled his chair to face the window behind him. People always talked about the beauty of space, but it wasn't beautiful. It was fierce, cruel and timeless. It was a killer of men and destroyer of ships. In all the vastness Garret had never felt so exposed.

The comms panel on his desk buzzed and grabbed back his attention. Whirling the chair, he knocked the glass from the desk and cursed under his breath. Perhaps he'd had one more than he should. Frowning, Garret pressed a couple of buttons and there was Underwood, glaring back at him.

'Captain.'

'Yes, Commander, what do you need?' The words were only very slightly slurred but it was perceptible to someone like Underwood, whose father had often wandered back to their apartment in Silver City after business meetings with the same slur and a strong smell of alcohol. She was grateful that their current communication was not face to face.

'I have had word back from the navigation deck. With our current engine power, the journey to these coordinates will take three months.'

'Thank you, Underwood.'

Garret ended their comms session. Three months. A lot could happen in three months, that much he knew from hard experience. Perhaps something would come up, something to prevent the need for the mission and save them all the pain of losing more people.

Garret picked up his drink and settled back to watching space pass him by.

***

When Alissa woke up the next morning it wasn't with a jump or a scream as she had grown accustomed to doing. It was with a long stretch and a satisfied sigh. She was grateful that there had been no nightmares. But then her dream came back to her, in fractured pieces and confusing snippets. This was new to her – since the tracker had been installed her dreams had been as clear as memories. Now they were fuzzy, and the more she tried to remember, the more they slipped away from her. She lay staring at the ceiling, trying to motivate herself to get up. Shem! He popped into her mind out of no-where, smiling and taking her by the hand. That's what she dreamed about ... Shem. But as she tried to remember, it was gone. In the end she didn't motivate herself into getting up – her bladder did.

As she went through her morning routine of picking up her uniform off the floor, tossing it onto the bed and wandering into the wet room for a shower. She thought about her dream. It infuriated her that the memory of it didn't exist in her. She missed Shem, the stubborn idiot. But she couldn't bring herself to see him again after the things he had said. And despite herself, she missed the dreams of Silver Glove, where she had vivid clarity and retention of the details. It pained her to think terrible things could be happening to him and there would be no way he could call for help – or worse, warn her of danger. That thought made the decision of where to start her day easy.

It would be a terrible thing to ask and she knew it. Garret would likely say no to her and that was fine, but she had to try. Pacing back and forth outside the captain's office, she felt like she would wear away the carpet, but starting this sort of conversation was impossible – she would pace back and forth out here until she thought of what to say.

There was really only one chance. If she failed, if he said no, then that would be it. Putting on her best chief of security face, Alissa pressed the panel and as the door slid open, she walked into the office.

The thing that really stood out was how rough Garret looked. It looked for all the world like he had sat in his chair, fallen asleep and spent the night there.

'Garret?'

He looked up at her standing over him and coughed to clear his throat.

'Alissa. What brings you here?'

Standing in front of his desk she picked at her uniform as if there was a loose thread. This wasn't what she expected; she needed to speak to a clear-headed Garret and now she felt ill at ease.

'It's okay, I can come back later.' She turned to leave.

'Alissa, sit down. Tell me why you're here.'

'Alright.' She turned to face him. 'I had a thought. And it worried me.' She crossed the room and sat in the chair opposite him.

'Was this thought related to the current trajectory of this ship?' This was Garret's way of deciding if it was something Underwood could be dealing with.

'Yes, sir. It is.'

Damn, was all he could think. Garret's head was pounding and his back ached from seven hours in his chair. The need to compose himself was urgent and he pulled himself up straight and looked Alissa in the eye.

'Then continue.'

'Captain, I want you to install the tracker back in my head.'

Garret's eyes opened wide. For what possible reason could this girl want the torment of those nightmares again? His confusion must've been apparent because Alissa continued:

'Garret, the man in my dreams was Silver Glove, but there were two versions of him. One with a Silver Glove and one without. I think the one without was trying to help us. He's the one I want to save.'

He sat silently. Alissa had hoped he would've said something by now, but he was going to let her say her entire piece before deciding.

'I think he would be a useful asset. A man on the inside who can warn us of any incoming threat. With the mission we're currently on, we need that.'

The two of them sat quietly for a few minutes more. Garret was waiting to see if there was anything she wanted to add, but she sat impassively, staring right back at him.

'Okay. I'll send word to Doctor Harper.'

The shock on Alissa's face must have been evident because Garret frowned.

'Is there something you're not telling me?'

'No! It's just ... I expected more of a fight.'

Garret smiled a wry smile. 'Truth be told Alissa, I've been thinking the same thing about the tracker. That having a connection to the hostiles could benefit us greatly.'

Relief flooded over her as she left Garret's office, and she smiled to herself. She would make sure Silver Glove was okay; he would help them protect the ship from afar; and she would save him from whatever torture he was being subjected to.

***

As Alissa headed to her office, Ham was walking into the prison sector once more. It had been tough on him, having to split time between Alissa and Shem. He didn't really understand why they were so angry at each other and he didn't know how to get them to fix it, so instead he just kept going between them, not mentioning one to the other unless they asked, just trying to enjoy their company as best he could.

Arriving at the cell, Ham peered inside as the field melted away. Shem smiled and got to his feet.

'Hey buddy, how's it going?' Ham always asked the same question and Shem always answered the same way – with a chuckle and a hug. They took their usual positions, Shem sitting on the bed and Ham on the bench facing him.

'So tell me, what am I missing out there? Anything good?'

Ham shook his head. 'Nothing I can talk about, really. Usual stuff.'

Shem frowned. 'Alissa stuff? About Silver Glove?'

Ham's face brightened. 'You know about that?'

Shem nodded. Alissa had told him everything.

'How is she? Is she okay?'

Ham's face darkened. 'I don't know, Shem. They put a tracker in her brain, those men. Made her dream about Silver Glove. They've been making her believe stuff all this time.'

The colour drained from Shem's face and he started to feel a little queasy.

'They've been manipulating her this whole time, haven't they?'

It took Ham a second, but he nodded.

All this time, they had still been exercising their power over her, torturing her really, and here he was, playing the part of a hurt puppy who nobody loved. For a moment he considered fleeing his cell and running straight to her, telling her everything was okay and that he understood now. But the idea of her frogmarching him back here was a humiliation even Shem couldn't take.

'Will you watch out for her? Take care of her?' Shem was almost pleading with Ham. 'She'll never admit it, but she needs us. Right now, all I can do is ask you to be there for her, no matter what she does. Okay?'

Ham nodded again. Things would get back to normal one day, he told himself. But even he was smart enough to know that probably wasn't true.

***

Alissa sat on her bed reading her comms pad, silly stories she had enjoyed as a child about monsters in caves and a little girl who wanted to be an adventurer. Growing up she had wanted to be a hero. Now here she sat, a woman, a murderer and a fool.

In an attempt to shake the thoughts away, Alissa stood up and jogged on the spot for a minute. She was delaying going to sleep as it was her first night with the tracker reinstalled, and no one really knew if it would work or if he would even appear to her. And she was scared. She walked to the basin in the wet room, turned on the tap and allowed the cool water to flow over her hands, gently washing away the day from her skin. She filled the glass that lived on the basin and drained it in one. It had been two hours since she had first decided to turn in; now it was time to sleep, and her stomach fluttered with nerves.

Heading back to her bed, she dropped her uniform on the floor in a trail behind her, picked up an old t-shirt from the carpet and tugged it over her head. Lying there, forcing herself to close her eyes, it took longer than she expected but eventually she drifted off into a deep sleep.

Silver Glove was waiting for her. Sitting in a darkened room at the end of a long table with his hands clenched together on the surface. She could see the shine of the metal hand in the dim light and the cruel look in his eye that he was trying to mask with that smile. Alissa sat on the cold stone floor and a shiver ran through her. She was still only in her t-shirt and the room was frigid. But he didn't seem to mind the cold.

He stood, a little too quickly, and started to walk around the table. Alissa watched, frozen to the spot as he got closer to her. This wasn't the Silver Glove she wanted to see. This Silver Glove wanted to hurt her – she could feel the loathing emanating from him. She rose to her feet, standing defiantly as he came closer. With each step the urge to turn and run was overwhelming, but she had asked for this, for the dreams to return, and she would fight every night if she had to, until she saw the man without the glove.

Closer and closer he came but Alissa stood her ground. She faced him without flinching until he was so close that she was sure he would hear the staccato beating of her heart. Adrenaline was pumping through her veins; every muscle was tensed and she was ready to pounce the moment he made a move. This time she would win. She had the same advantage he did: she too knew it was a dream.

132

'Tell me, when did you get so brave?' His silken voice, like caramel, enveloped her. But it did not have the usual impact. His eyes narrowed at her bravery and her silence.

'Perhaps I ought to remind you why you fear me.'

His hand reached into his jacket very slowly. Alissa didn't take her eyes from his. She knew what was coming and she was ready for it. He traced the blade down her cheek, and she felt the smallest trickle of warm blood.

Alissa pulled away and used her left arm to knock back his silver hand, sending the knife tumbling to the floor.

'I'm coming to kill you.'

These were the only words that escaped her lips before she found herself back in her own bed.

A night of fitful sleep was all Alissa managed before meeting Ham for breakfast in the Rec. It felt like so many years had passed since she had found Stadler in here – decades since Shem's fight with Ryan. With all she was learning about alien life and technology, Alissa wondered if there existed a time machine; she could use it to change everything. To go back to the aptitude test and study, prepare herself properly and get on the Ark without Silver Glove. Although if she had, then someone else would've been drafted and perhaps they would have succeeded in killing Clarke Andover, leaving the Ark open to attack. Perhaps they would all already be dead.

This grim line of thinking was swirling around Alissa's mind as Ham arrived and sat himself beside her at the table. Giving her his best smile, he picked up the plastic menu from the table.

'Hey Ham. You hungry?'

He nodded vigorously. 'Starved. I've not had a good meal in days with all the work I've been doing.'

'Why so busy?'

Ham looked at her a little sheepishly. 'With all the stuff I was doing with you and Garret and stuff, I got behind with ship repairs. Plus, I've been going to see Shem a lot. He gets kinda lonely down there.'

Alissa felt a pang of guilt. She still hadn't seen him since their fight and selfishly hadn't really given thought to the impact that would have. Shem was a bit of a pariah on the Ark; no one wanted to visit him except Ham and Alissa. And since she had stopped her visits, Ham was all he had.

'I'm sorry. I've not been a great friend recently.' She meant every word.

Ham shrugged and looked up from the menu. 'I want one of those burgers – they say they've actually got them to taste good now!'

Alissa smiled and decided on the same. She went to the bar to order, glancing over at Ham while she waited. Her heart broke for him, stuck in the middle, being dragged from place to place, working far harder than any other technician and getting no respect for it. Anger started to bubble in her gut for the life he was living, and she decided right then that no matter what, she would spend as much time with Ham as she possibly could.

When she went back to the table Ham was flipping bar mats off the edge of the table and catching them.

'I can do eight at the most. More than that and they scatter everywhere.'

He chuckled as Alissa grabbed a few from neighbouring tables and joined in, flipping around five before she dropped them all.

'Shem wants me to take care of you, Alissa ...'

134

She froze, holding a fistful of mats and staring at the table.

'... But I don't know how because you keep going to Garret and doing secret alien stuff.'

She gently placed the mats on the table and turned to face Ham.

'I know things are hard right now, Ham. And the day will come when I can tell you everything. But for now, I need you to take care of me when I'm not working. Because I get lost in it.'

Self-reflection was something she had always avoided but the fact was, since the dreams, she never turned off from work. Never stopped thinking about the ship, or Garret or Silver Glove. She was constantly on edge and desperately afraid. Eventually something had to break, and she was terrified every day that it would be her.

CHAPTER NINETEEN

'ALISSA? CAN YOU HEAR ME?' THE FLOOR WAS   beneath her. Why was she lying down? Her head swam and she opened her eyes and tried to turn round. The light of the place blinded her, the burn of sunlight, and she squinted away from it. Then came his voice again.

'Alissa, come on, you have to get up.'

It was Silver Glove. He was helping her to her feet, and with his arms around her waist the first thing she noticed was his human hands. His flesh and bone hands.

They were standing on a dusty plain looking out over a desert. The air was stuffy and hot and stung Alissa's face. She grabbed his hands and turned them over in her own.

'Who are you?' She shook her head as she spoke. 'Why is your hand ... like this?' She lifted his arm slightly as if to emphasise her question.

'My name is Japheth.'

Alissa faltered for a moment; this man had a name.

'What?' she whispered.

'Japheth.'

'How are you doing this?' She motioned around them. 'How are you in my head?'

Japheth took a deep breath, his face was filled with concern. He seemed ready to cry. She had never seen him look so dishevelled, so real.

'I was born on Earth, like you. But I was taken by them' – he motioned upwards – 'and they used me like a puppet, took my face and my personality, the very essence of me, and they installed it into a machine. They used it to project him. But we're connected, I see everything through his eyes. I saw you.'

Alissa stood in disbelief as he continued:

'I don't have a lot of time to explain, but I can use the tracker to reach out to you, when I'm not being used by them.'

Japheth had the haunted look of a man who had been broken, but there was still fight left in him and Alissa was prepared, now more than ever, to risk everything to save him. Because for the first time, she was seeing his real humanity and he deserved her help – *their* help.

***

The dreams continued each night and Alissa was defiant when faced with Silver Glove, and gentle when Japheth managed to come through to her. She and Japheth took time to learn about each other, talking about their families and their lives back on Earth. Japheth had lived in a small complex close to New Amerland called Germanus. She had heard of it – apparently the first man to take charge was of German decent and wished to honour his heritage. Most of the people were just focused on surviving, so no one questioned him. Japheth had worked as an educator; he was one of the people responsible for overseeing the Germanus aptitude test. He himself had failed and so was destined to die with so many others. The irony wasn't lost on Alissa and she gave a bitter laugh.

The time she was spending with him was fulfilling for her. He was a man who cared about her, listened to her stories and said no harsh words. She wasn't judged by him. She even found herself talking about her relationship, and its complicated nature, with Shem. And he listened and told her about his sister who had been born with an illness that plagued her life. He cared for her through their teenage years and into adulthood. After he was taken, he always wondered what became of her and it broke his heart to think of it. Worse still, he would never be able to go back and find her. He just hoped that someone, somewhere, had taken her in and looked after her.

It had only been a week since the tracker had been reinstalled, but it felt much longer to Alissa. She looked on Japheth as an old friend, and always looked forward to falling asleep in the hopes that she would see him.

***

One of the conditions of the reinstallation of the transmitter was that Alissa would report to Garret weekly with updates on the dreams, and to reveal any information that was relevant to the mission they had given themselves.

Alissa was sat in her office, shifting uncomfortably as she considered what the day would hold for her. The conversation with Ham that she had rehearsed in her head was something that she dreaded to her very core, but it was the right choice to make. She checked the time; it was nine in the morning and Ham would just be starting his shift. It's now or never, she told herself.

***

Garret was on the bridge. It was rare that he ventured here since it reminded him of Clarke. This was his place and Garret felt for all the world like a cheap imitation and he hated it. For the first time since he received his promotion, he seated himself in the captain's seat and looked out at the sea of blackness stretching out before him. The full front of the room was an interactive window space. It not only showed the view; it could zoom in on objects and show them in perfect clarity. It also served as a video relay during communications and allowed most ship systems to run through it. The idea was that N.O.A.H. could scan and target any number of objects, relay the information to the nav deck and avoid a level-critical incident.

There were only three officers working on the main bridge at any given time and today's contingent were mostly unknown to Garret. He believed the nav officer was Isla; there was an engineering chief monitoring the ship's wellbeing, whose name escaped Garret, and a security officer called Mercer. They sat in silence with Garret watching space go by, trying to forget the situation they were in and enjoy the stars the way he used to.

***

'Noah, please tell me where Ham is.'

Alissa was zipping up her boots. She had a tendency to kick them off and let her feet enjoy the warm beige carpet, sliding them over the fuzzy surface or wiggling her toes into it.

'Please clarify. Ham?'

Alissa frowned, then remembered why she didn't use N.O.A.H. to find Ham. Ham's real name was known to only a select few. His parents had given him the nickname after his grandfather had found him up to his eyeballs in packaged fake-meat products, his cheeks packed and a guilty look on his face. The name had stuck and fortunately he quite liked it; he said it made him feel special.

'Okay, Noah. Please tell me where ... Aristotle Windsor is currently located.'

His parents had thought themselves very fancy. They insisted that they were descended from the British monarchy and made sure that was reflected in the name of every family member.

The masculine computer voice responded, 'Aristotle Windsor is currently in Tech Lab Three.'

'Thanks Noah!' Alissa called out as she left the room.

'You are welcome,' came the robotic reply.

At the tech lab, Alissa stood in the open doorway for a few minutes, leaning on the wooden frame with her arms folded, watching Ham work. It was evident to her that he wasn't enhanced right now and yet his hands worked masterfully over the engine parts he was manipulating, and the focus on his face was clear. Alissa watched as a proud mother would. No one ever saw Ham like this – he lost all confidence when people were around. People were cruel. She saw how remarks could cut him and wished she could wrap him up and keep him safe. Instead she was going to ask him to help her on a suicide mission and he was going to say yes because he cared so much.

Ham, for his part, was having a moment. Sometimes, he thought, you can just tell you're not alone – you know

140

you're being watched. That's how he felt right then, so he glanced over his shoulder and smiled when he saw Alissa standing in the doorway.

'Hey!'

His enthusiastic greeting was accompanied by an even more enthusiastic waving of the hand. Alissa smiled in return, but to Ham she still looked sad.

'What's the matter? Are you still upset about Shem?'

The question clearly caught her off guard. She muttered about it not being important while she scuffed her boot to and fro on the carpet.

There was an empty chair next to Ham and she claimed it, turning it sideways to get comfy.

'Ham, I need you to do something for me.'

He went back to working on his engine part and nodded. 'Sure, what d'ya need?'

'Well, I need to you come on a mission with me.'

Ham looked up. 'Go on a mission? There's nowhere to go.'

'Well, ordinarily that would be true. But we are on a journey to meet with a potentially hostile alien life form, and I need to go to them, find Japheth and save him.' Ham's face was a picture of confusion as she continued: 'They are responsible for all the bad stuff that's happened since I got taken. We need to talk to them, try and make them see that we mean no harm to anyone.'

Ham was looking at the part in his hands and turning it over. Shem had made him promise to take care of Alissa no matter what. But this was scary. He remembered the little boy pointing the gun at him, and remembered how terrified he was. He never wanted to feel that way again. But Alissa needed him.

'Alissa, I can't. I've none of the drugs left.'

'Ham, you are smarter and better than anyone else on this ship. Nothing gets past you when it comes to tech. You're the only one who will understand their technology and I might need that.' Then she took a deep breath and released it in a whoosh. 'But Ham, it's gonna be dangerous. We might both die.'

He thought of his promise to Shem. 'Okay Alissa. I'll go with you, but on one condition.'

Alissa raised her eyebrows. 'And what's that?'

'I want to tell Shem.'

Alissa stiffened. She couldn't let knowledge of the mission spread around the ship, but Ham was right – Shem would need to know. He deserved to know. Without saying another word, Alissa nodded.

CHAPTER TWENTY

GARRET HAD A LOT TO SAY ABOUT ALISSA'S ACTIONS and behaviour. Explaining the mission to Ham was one thing – he needed to understand exactly what was at risk. But to let him tell a prisoner was altogether unacceptable.

'How could you be so stupid, Alissa?'

Garret was pacing. His voice was low but shaking. It was clear he was trying to control his temper and Alissa hated what she was seeing. But she sat silently, allowing him to continue.

'I can't understand why you would allow a security risk like this one. You're irresponsible, and you consistently put your own feelings before the welfare of this ship.'

Her silence was annoying him so she kept it up. Eventually, he sat down and looked at her.

'Tell me why, Alissa.'

Calmly Alissa uncrossed her legs and leaned forward, resting her arms on the table.

143

'We need a good pilot, Garret. Think about it.'

***

Shem and Ham sat beside each other on the bench in the cell. Shem was staring at the wall in disbelief.

'You're both going.'

It was a statement, not a question. His two closest friends were leaving the Ark to fight aliens and probably die.

'Do you think there is a scenario in which I wouldn't move the Earth to come with you?'

Ham's shoulders slumped. This is something he was desperately afraid of. He didn't want Shem to be in danger and he couldn't look after them both.

'Shem, no. Don't even think about it. Anyway, for obvious reasons you can't.'

'Bullshit.' Shem spat the word out and leapt to his feet. 'You're supposed to be watching over her, and now you tell me you're going on a suicide mission? This is bullshit, Ham!'

Shem was almost yelling as he paced around the tiny room. Ham, on the other hand, had gone very quiet. He lifted his feet onto the bench and hugged his knees while his eyes followed Shem round the room. It took a few minutes before Shem realised the position his friend was in and when he did, it was like being punched in the gut.

'Man, I'm sorry, Ham.' Shem had stopped right in the centre of the cell and was staring at the door. 'I've never had anyone in my life like you. Or Alissa. I don't think people like you two even exist anywhere else.' He slowly walked back to the bench and sat down. 'If my choice is to die with you or live the rest of my life without you guys then ...'

144

Ham knew the rest. After all, he was doing the same for Alissa, protecting her from whoever or whatever may want to hurt her, albeit the only way he would be any use to anyone would be with the enhancers. He started to tear up as he remembered that the last packet was used to work on the implant device.

'I need to speak to Garret,' said Shem.

Ham nodded in response and they stood up together. It occurred to Ham that if Garret said no then this would probably be the last time he saw Shem. He turned and hugged his friend tight. Moments like this weren't easy for him and he tried not to be upset, but the tears fell, and he felt ashamed.

Shem, on the other hand, held Ham with nothing but pure affection. He understood what Ham was feeling and would give him the last memory he deserved.

***

'I'm sorry Shem, but it's protocol.'

Alissa stepped behind Shem as he shook his head in disbelief. The handcuffs weren't exactly uncomfortable, but it was the humiliation that hurt. Being in a cell was one thing but being paraded around the ship in handcuffs was altogether more distressing.

'I get it Alissa.'

It was the first words they had spoken since the argument. Alissa wasn't best pleased when Garret sent her personally to get Shem; she had the feeling it would happen but to be living the moment she dreaded was awful. She felt like the executioner taking the condemned man to his final destination.

Once the cuffs were in place Shem turned to face Alissa.

'Talk to me, Al.'

His eyes were pleading, but Alissa couldn't let this get personal; she was on duty. She thought back to the day he punched Ryan and wondered how it had all come to this.

'Come on, I need to get you to Garret.'

When they arrived at the office Garret and Underwood were waiting. Alissa walked Shem in and sat him down in the chair facing Garret.

'Thank you, Alissa. You're excused.'

For a second the words didn't register. She had just assumed she would be here for the meeting, since she was the commanding officer for the mission. And since it was her idea in the first place. When she finally found the words, they tumbled out quicker and less professionally than she had hoped.

'Wait, what? No, I'm staying for this, Garret.'

'Alissa, I have made a great many allowances for you and your friends for obvious reasons.' He paused his usual long pause and Alissa wanted to scream. 'However, this is a conflict of interest for you.'

She just started at him open-mouthed. To be fair, she wasn't used to being told no and had grown accustomed to the freedoms she had been afforded. Looking around the office she saw Underwood, and her face explained it all. She has been whispering in Garret's ear – the perfect new first officer, who clearly disliked Alissa.

'Fine.' It was supposed to sound nonchalant but instead was dripping with hurt. She turned on her heel and left the room.

***

'Alright Mr Mitchell, you wanted a meeting with me. Please state your reason.'

As Garret spoke, Underwood took up a comms pad, set it to record and placed it on the desk between Garret and Shem.

Clearing his throat, Shem began the speech he had been rehearsing.

'First of all, I want to thank you for agreeing to see me. And for letting me fight my corner here.' He was nervous and his mouth was drying up as he spoke. He coughed, and Alice presented him with a glass of water from which he took a long drink. Garret nodded for him to continue.

'I have made mistakes on this ship and I've currently got a lot of time to think about them. There are so many things I wish I could go back and change but that's not possible. So instead I want to make a difference now. I know about the mission and I want to go.'

Garret raised an eyebrow but remained silent.

'I'm expendable, sir. I'm in prison and when I do get out, I'll be a cleaner. I'm not needed here anymore. So, don't let me disappear into nothing. Give me the chance to atone.'

Garret now took the opportunity to ask what was on his mind. 'This is all very selfless of you. The mission is one of peace and diplomacy, but within a hostile environment. You may very well simply be shot on sight. What are you asking for in return?'

Shem looked down. 'I want my friends back. I don't want anything from you, sir.'

CHAPTER TWENTY-ONE

THE REMAINDER OF THE JOURNEY WAS SPENT   train-ing. Shem was temporarily released on the understand-ing that while he wasn't in training he would be confined to quarters. This suited the three friends perfectly, and it was strange how easily they fell back into an easy cama-raderie. Shem and Alissa never spoke again about their fight and instead focused on rebuilding what they had once had.

The night before they were due to reach the coordi-nates, Alissa's comms pad bleeped with a message. It was an invite to a fancy dinner at Shem's quarters, with the specific instruction that it was black tie. She laughed at the thought of Ham and Shem in suits.

She went immediately to Megan's. The doctor was around four months gone and showing a lovely little bump. Alissa smiled as she was invited into Megan's room. Garret had insisted on staying in his own quar-ters, which left the captain's free for Megan.

'I need a dress!' Alissa surprised herself by just blurting it out. 'Sorry, I mean … well, how are you?'

Megan laughed. 'It's fine. I'm great, baby is doing great. What kind of dress?'

'I don't know. I don't own one.'

'Well, what do you need it for?'

Alissa flashed her invite and Megan smiled. 'Going on a date, are we?'

'What? No! Shem's having a party for the three of us – me, Shem and Ham.'

'Okay, Al.' Megan began pulling dresses out of her closet. 'I've got the perfect one.'

Megan was kind enough to help Alissa get ready for the night. She curled her long, brown hair and pinned it up, with just a few delicate curls falling to her shoulders. The make-up took a little while to get right. Alissa was a mascara only kind of girl, but Megan had other plans. She rouged her cheeks, lined her eyes and carefully applied a beautiful shade of red to her lips, which matched the dress perfectly.

The dress was a floor-length affair, with a low neck. It clung to Alissa in the right places and Megan grinned with satisfaction when they had finished. She even managed to get the security chief into heels, no easy task. Alissa stood in front of the mirror looking at her new reflection. It was certainly a different look for her and one she wasn't sure about. The shoes pinched her toes and the thin straps of the dress rubbed her shoulders, but politely she said:

'Thanks, Meg.'

***

The door chime rang out and Shem took a deep, calming breath. He was nervous about to tonight but excited. The mere fact that she had accepted the invitation was proof enough for him that the fight really was over. The lights in his quarters were dimmer than usual, and a warm glow was offered by an array of candles on the table – a table set only for two. There was soft music playing and the air was filled with a beautiful floral scent. Shem stepped across the room and pressed the panel to open the door.

'This,' he said under his breath, 'is a *date*.'

The door slid silently back and there stood Alissa. As she stepped in he gave a little gasp.

'You look amazing, Al.'

She looked nervously down at herself. 'Right back at you.'

She grinned, turned a chair sideways to sit by the table, and looked at Shem. Gone was the stubble from his time in the prison sector, his hair had been styled – and she had to admit he looked good in a suit.

'So, what're we having?'

'A vegetable moussaka. I had it delivered in from the civ sector. Even got us a bottle of wine.' Shem had developed quite the taste for wine since their meal all those months ago. Before he went to prison, he would order in a bottle every week or so.

'Sounds good to me.'

They sat in silence for a few minutes, the music wafting around them as they looked at their hands, and their napkins, and their cutlery. Finally, Alissa spoke.

'Why did you ask me here, Shem?'

That made the mood even more awkward for both of them.

'Okay. Look, you know how I feel about you.' He nervously rubbed at his brow while he spoke, unable to look Alissa in the eye. 'I think I've made it quite clear that for the last five years I've been in love with you. Now, there's a real risk that we might die tomorrow, and I didn't want to die having never taken you on a date – or told you how I feel.'

He looked up at her to gauge her reaction. Her expression was soft as her eyes met his.

'You know, I think you might be right – about tomorrow.' She reached out and took him by the hand. 'So, on with the date then.'

Shem raised an eyebrow.

'I mean feed me the moussaka!'

She laughed as he jumped to his feet. When he came back to the table he was carrying two metallic serving platters, both piled high and smelling wonderful. He placed one at each of their seats, then went to retrieve the wine.

The moussaka was incredible, which was good since they were both eating it like it was their last meal. The wine flowed nicely alongside it and by the end of the meal they were both laughing at memories shared and good times had before the Ark, and the four men, and the aptitude test.

All too soon for both of them, the night came to an end when Alissa's alarm went off.

'We have eight hours before we launch.' She put the comms back in her purse. 'I should really go.'

Ever the gentleman, Shem escorted her across the room to the door.

'Under normal circumstances I'd walk you home.'

Alissa stood on the threshold, looking up at Shem. He leaned in and gave her a kiss on the cheek. She smiled up at him, then turned and walked down the corridor. Shem watched until she had turned the corner. Then he closed the door, blew out the candles, and went to bed.

CHAPTER TWENTY-TWO

'THERE'S NOTHING THERE.' GARRET FROWNED AS he stared out of the viewscreen into the vast blackness of space. They had stopped the ship twenty-four hours short of the coordinates and, they hoped, out of the range of most scanners. They had performed an overnight scan and found the area completely vacant. Admittedly, Garret wasn't overwhelmed with disappointment at the lack of ship or data at the specified coordinates. In fact, it was a relief to him. He hoped that perhaps the aliens had picked a fight elsewhere and had gotten themselves destroyed.

After Garret spoke, none of the crew were willing to break the silence and risk provoking the new captain. For a few moments more, Garret watched the nothingness outside. Then he reached for his comms to contact Alissa.

***

It had been an early start for the security chief. Already she had showered, dressed and strapped up her heavy boots. With each passing moment more knots tied themselves into her stomach and she honestly felt like throwing up. The nerves were going to put an end to her mission before it even began unless she sorted herself out. Megan had taught Alissa some calming techniques during their sessions and now seemed like as good a time as any to give them a try. There was quiet in the room, except for the gentle hum of the engines. The techs on board had managed to increase engine capacity since the explosion and their speed had increased slightly.

Sitting on the floor, her legs crossed, Alissa closed her eyes and let her mind go blank. There was to be nothing disturbing her. Just Alissa with her own heartbeat.

Then the comms buzzed and the screen came to life.

She grumbled quietly as she crossed the room and answered the call. Looking back at her was Garret.

'Alissa, I have some news.'

***

Ham was sitting in the Rec eating a sandwich. He had decided to fill up before the mission and he'd struggled to sleep the night before so had spent most of that time eating. The nice lady behind the counter brought him another mug of coffee and smiled kindly as she put it down beside him. Ham watched her walk away. A plumpish girl, probably only a year or two older than himself. Her eyes were kind and the coffee she made was really good. Ham smiled to himself as he took another bite of his sandwich.

The Rec was quiet at this time in the morning. No one wanted to wander the ship so early unless they were on shift, and even then, they rarely went to the Rec while on the job. It was definitely an after-hours place and since the night shift didn't finish for another hour, it would remain quiet. Just as Ham stuffed the last few bites into his mouth, his comms pad chirped in his pocket. He pulled it out and answered. It was Garret.

**

Shem sat on the chair where only the night before he'd been laughing over candlelight with Alissa. Now the room was silent, but he could still hear Garret's words ringing in his ears. The mission was cancelled. He pressed the heels of his hands into his eyes and choked back a sob. He was trying so hard to fix his life but now he would be right back where he started. In prison for being an idiot and the worst nav chief that ever lived.

From across the room his panel chimed again and he dragged himself over to answer it. This time the face filling the screen was Alissa's.

'Hey Shem, have you heard from Garret?'

Shem laughed bitterly.

'Yeah. I'm just waiting for a security detail to escort me back to the cell.'

There was silence as Alissa stared at him open-mouthed. Finally, she said:

'No, Shem. If there was a team coming to you, I would know about it. I'm the chief remember?'

'I don't think Garret trusts you with this one, Al.'

'Wait there.'

The terminal went blank.

***

By the time Alissa had run the seven corridors separating her from Shem, he was already gone. His quarters were eerily – ominously – quiet. Last night the place had been filled with such joy and laughter. In the harshness of the morning hour, it was cold and lonely, and Shem was gone.

With her jaw set and her hands balled into fists, Alissa stormed onto the bridge of the Ark, not stopping until she was standing over Garret. His eyes widened and he raised his hand, as though he thought she might hit him.

'You promised him. You gave him back his freedom and you can't take it away now. It's not fair and as chief of security, I won't allow it.' Her voice was raised, and she was leaning closer to Garret with every word.

Garret rose to his feet and looked his chief in the eye.

'Alissa, you don't decide what happens on this ship. I do.' He turned away and walked towards the door, stopping only as the door slid open to say, 'I am the captain now. It's about time you respected that.'

'Garret, don't walk away from me.'

He didn't break stride as he ignored Alissa's plea, leaving her standing awkwardly on the bridge.

***

Ham was happy. Relief had flooded him the instant he heard about the mission falling through. He practically skipped back to his quarters and sat on the edge of his bed. Within minutes he was on his back, snoring loudly.

***

156

Shem stared straight ahead as he was led back to his cell. On the walk down he hadn't seen Alissa, which he assumed meant she had gone to Garret. It wouldn't help him, he knew that. His return here was on Garret's orders. The cell hadn't changed – it was still grim and bare.

***

Alissa sat in her office, staring at the monitor in front of her and trying to take deep, calming breaths – but it was hardly working. She was mad. Mad at Garret for throwing Shem in a cell and humiliating her on the bridge, mad at Silver Glove for lying to her, but mostly mad at herself for believing in monsters. Silver Glove did this to her to torment her. She knew that now, and she wouldn't let it happen again.

If this was all some alien ploy to abuse her then she would have the last laugh. Alissa stood. Her mind was made up. As chief of security, she was going to get Shem out of prison.

***

Garret had made his way back to the bridge after his dramatic exit. It had reached a point where Alissa needed to learn her place on board this ship. He stared into the black sea before him and thought about how to teach her to be a more disciplined chief. It was time she stopped focusing so much on herself and her friends. Now she would have to focus on the ship and its crew. Otherwise she would find herself back on mechanic duties.

While he keyed through some data on his comms pad, a mousy-looking woman appeared on the screen. She cleared her throat.

'Captain, I think ... well, I think I've found something ... odd.'

She was small and slender, with short brown hair. It occurred to Garret, not for the first time, that you had to be twenty-five to take the test and get a job with the crew, but that this girl looked so much younger than that.

'What've you found, Claire?'

'Well, I'm not sure, Captain.'

Garret raised an eyebrow and Claire's eyes widened a little in response.

'I just mean, I've never seen anything like it. The readings are all over the place, but—'

'Spit it out, girl.'

'There's two sets of data for the same area of space, sir.'

Garret's face went slowly from confusion to concern.

'She's right sir,' Lt. Cole chimed in. 'I'm getting results on the long-range scan that shows readings consistent with where we are – standard background radiation and other indicators, all what we'd expect to see. But there's a small area that's anomalous. It's giving me radiation readings consistent with ringed planets. If I didn't know better, I'd say there was a Saturn-similar planet right at these coordinates.'

Garret turned back to the viewscreen and stared into the same blackness. Just empty space; he could see that it was empty space. And yet, there was a planet there? It didn't make sense.

'Alright, hold our position here. Send out the long-range probe. But be careful with it, we only have the one.'

Cole nodded as Garret rose to his feet.

'I'll be in my office. Update me once you have something.'

With that, he left the bridge.

***

When Alissa arrived at the prison, the duty officer smiled and stood a little straighter.

'Chief? Is there something you need?'

Alissa barely glanced at the officer and started tapping keys until she saw details of Shem and which cell he was in.

'I need Shem Mitchell releasing immediately. Please take care of the paperwork for me while I escort him out.' Alissa turned towards the cell corridors.

'I'm sorry Chief, I can't do that.'

'Excuse me?'

'Captain's orders, Sir. Shem Mitchell can only be released on his orders. Not yours.'

Alissa's shoulders stiffened. Garret thought he had her beat. But she had no intention of giving way. She would find a way to release Shem and ... Then what? There was nowhere for them to run.

'Open the door. Surely I'm still able to see him?'

The door clicked and Alissa pushed it open, walking down the long corridor and peering into Shem's cell. He looked okay. Not happy but not as dismayed as before. As the field between them fell away she walked into his cell, taking him in her arms and just holding him where they stood.

CHAPTER TWENTY-THREE

'CAPTAIN, WE'VE FOUND SOMETHING.' COLE'S VOICE was a dull thud in Garret's silence. The captain rose to his feet and slowly walked to the bridge. Once there he sat in his chair and waited for an explanation.

'Well, sir, the probe was released towards the coordinates, all scans were nominal, and the probe was in visual range. Until it wasn't.'

'What do you mean, until it wasn't?'

'Sir, the probe vanished when it hit the co-ords. However, it is still transmitting data back to us. It seems to have travelled alright, sir. To an uncharted section of the universe.'

Garret stared hard out of the viewscreen.

'And how, exactly, did it travel that far?'

'Sir.' It was Claire. 'Sir, I believe it's a wormhole.'

***

Garret was back in his office. A *wormhole*? Was that even possible? Had Alissa been right? He had secretly hoped that their alien conspiracy was all invented. Or at least that the circumstances that had been misunder-stood. But now … now he knew for certain – whatever or whoever had brought them here intended for them to travel through the rip in space/time and meet them on their own territory.

***

Alissa was still in Shem's cell, sitting on the bunk with her friends. Ham had made his way down once he woke up and the three of them were catching up. Alissa hadn't laughed this much in a long time; there was no drama, no pressure, just good memories and a feeling of relief – at least for Alissa and Ham. Then Alissa's comms pad bleeped. It was Garret.

***

Garret was on the bridge when Alissa arrived. All eyes turned to her.

'So, what do we do, Captain?'

'I believe we should go in. It appears to be a relative-ly safe journey and our probe tells us there are no ships waiting on the other side.'

Alissa nodded and Garret put out the word to the crew and guests. All were advised to strap themselves into the safety seats located in their quarters or in the public areas. The bridge crew duly strapped in – all ex-cept Garret and Alissa, who remained standing.

Garret gave the order, and slowly the ship pulled forward, towards the wormhole.

It was a rocky journey that lasted just a few minutes. At first, everything outside the ship was cloaked in a dull and lifeless grey. But the ship rode on, and suddenly there were stars and space once more. Even a ringed planet. It was a once-in-a-lifetime experience. And one Garret hoped to repeat on the return journey.

But that was all. There was nothing else to be seen and Alissa felt her stomach sink. There should be something here, some form of ship. Japheth or Silver Glove – or whoever he was – should be here waiting.

The bridge crew sat at their posts in stunned silence. They were the first Earth vessel to travel through a wormhole, and the gravity of the moment didn't escape a single one of them.

Except Alissa.

'Why is there no one here, Garret? What did we do wrong?'

He didn't immediately respond, but continued to stare out into space. He was looking at the vast darkness, the unfamiliar stars, the new planet, and Alissa would have to wait – there were more important things to deal with. Finally, Garret said:

'Right helm. Keep us steady and manoeuvre us into a low orbit around the ringed planet. It'll hide us from a lot of sensors but be ready with the gas pedal. We might have to get out of here fast and I want to be ready if we do.'

Garret turned on his heel while Alissa stared daggers at him. He ignored her and addressed the assembled tactical team. 'Please keep a long-range scan sweeping the area. If anything comes into range, I want to know what it is, who's manning it and why they're here.'

Alissa watched as Garret walked the bridge, barking commands at his crew and watching them jump into action. All this time, even after assuming command, she had seen Garret as she had always seen him; but this was something new to her. He was the captain of this ship, and she was his security chief. She stood a little straighter as he made his way over to her.

'Alissa, alert your entire team. I want everyone on standby until we know the ship isn't in any danger. Should a raiding party come on board, I need to know you're ready to handle it.'

'Yes, sir.' She saluted, and immediately regretted it. Garret raised an eyebrow and nodded at her. Alissa turned tail and left the bridge.

***

The day had been long and exhausting. Alissa lay her head down and finally closed her eyes. After leaving the bridge, she had spent the day running emergency drills with her teams. They over performed in every test and Alissa felt a little swell of pride.

She was physically and mentally drained, and it could only have been seconds before she was fast asleep. A hand gently stroked her cheek while she slept, rousing her back to the waking world and gently saying her name.

'Alissa.'

She groaned and rolled away. 'Just let me have a few more minutes, my alarm hasn't even gone off yet.'

There was a gentle laugh and Alissa opened her eyes. There on the edge of her bed was Japheth, flesh and blood hand still hovering where her cheek had been. She sat up in bed, covering herself with the sheets, and blinked the sleep away from her eyes.

'We came to find you. To save you. Why aren't you here?'

'They want your ship, Alissa. They want to kill every person on board.'

His voice was gentle, but the words made Alissa flinch.

'Why? I don't understand.'

'I don't know, because Silver Glove doesn't know.' He looked uncomfortable. 'Alissa, you have to go back. Turn around and go back through the wormhole. Get as far away from here as you can. Saving me isn't worth risking all the people on your ship.'

'I know.' Alissa's voice came out quieter than she was used to. 'But this goes beyond just you and me. They want to destroy humanity and I for one am not going to let them. If they're gonna hunt us down anyway, I say we go out fighting.'

The next words out of Japheth's mouth were numbers. A long series of numbers and letters. After he finished he took Alissa's hand.

'Remember that sequence. You'll need it.'

With a start, Alissa woke up. Throwing the sheet aside, she said, 'Noah, record.'

'Recording.'

Alissa blurted the numbers out as loud and clear as she could. 'Save recording, Noah.'

'Saved.'

Alissa had no idea why her first instinct wasn't to run to Garret. It felt like he wanted distance from her, and she could feel his annoyance with her every time she was near him. It was clear to her that he regretted his decision to promote her. In truth, he had been manipulated into it by the men in the Facility. Every aspect of her life was tainted by them; they would forever be a part of her.

With a shudder, Alissa checked the clock. It was still early, but not too early to see Shem. If there was one person that could make her feel the way she did back in New Amerland, it was Shem.

When she arrived at the prison sector, Bourne was on duty. She nodded and Bourne opened the door to Shem's cell block. In seconds she was at the door, smiling at Shem as he jumped out of bed.

'Morning!' She laughed and turned her back. Shem didn't wear much to bed and Alissa wasn't quite prepared for the view.

'Yeah, hey Al. Thanks for knocking.' A few awkward seconds passed. 'Okay, I'm good.'

He had pulled on some cotton pants and a sweater. Still yawning, he sat back down on the bed while Alissa took a seat on the bench. 'What's with the wake-up call?'

'I ... just wanted to hang out.' Alissa looked around the cell at nothing in particular.

'Uh-huh.' He didn't sound convinced.

'Okay, I'm actually a little freaked out and ... well, I wanted to distract myself.'

Even as she said the words, she regretted them. Shem looked visibly wounded and folded his arms across his chest.

'I didn't mean it like that. I just meant ... things are rough right now, and you're the person I want to be around because ...' Shem had leaned forward slightly, hanging on her words. 'Well, because you're my best friend, Shem.'

He crossed the tiny room and sat himself beside her on the bench, wrapped an arm around her shoulder and nodded.

'Yeah. I know.'

165

'I had another dream about him last night. He said all these numbers but wouldn't tell me why they lied to us, Shem.'

'You know I've never been great at puzzles.'

Alissa gently laughed. 'Yeah, you really suck.'

'Hey, I'm locked away and all you wanna do it come down here and throw insults at me? Alissa, I'm hurt.' He chuckled. 'So, what were the numbers?'

Alissa got N.O.A.H. to play her recording. Shem started to smile.

'Turns out I might be good at puzzles after all.'

'You know what they mean?'

'They're coordinates, Alissa.'

Within seconds, Alissa was on her feet, instructing N.O.A.H. to patch the recording through to Garret. He said he expected her imminent arrival on the bridge.

'I have to go.'

With that, she flung her arms around his neck and held him tight. He hugged her back, but whispered to her, 'This means it might still be on; we might still be destined for a suicide mission.'

'Maybe. But I'd rather die trying than give up and wait to be killed.'

***

'I was expecting you much sooner.'

Garret sounded calm but that was the flat tone he used when he was at his most annoyed.

Alissa stood beside him, looking out the viewscreen at the ringed planet.

'Alissa, the numbers you gave me were coordinates. You understand that, don't you?'

'Yes, sir.'

166

'And no one else knows about this?'

'No, sir.'

Garret grabbed her suddenly by the bicep and marched her to the meeting room at the back of the bridge. Once through the door he released her and closed the door behind them. Alissa rubbed her arm and stared at the floor.

'You're lucky I didn't respond, Garret. You're lucky I have more respect for you than that.'

He made a kind of half-guffaw at her words; clearly he was amused and exasperated at the same time and was desperately trying to control his anger.

'You are the most petulant child I have ever met in my life, Alissa.' He pointed at the chair beside where she stood. 'Sit!'

Alissa complied. Usually when Garret was angry it was easy to get through it, but this side of him was new to her.

'You are tracked everywhere you go on board this ship, Alissa. What about me makes you think that I'm not a thorough man?'

'Nothing, I—'

'The question was entirely rhetorical. Since I can't trust a thing you say, I think it would be wise for you to keep your mouth shut.' He began to pace. 'Over the comms, you told me you had dreamed these numbers. According to Noah, you left your room this morning and practically ran to the prison sector to see Mr Mitchell.'

'Garret, I was just—'

He held up his hand. 'Again I say to you, I trust nothing that comes out of your mouth.' He lowered his arm and went back to pacing.

'The mission will happen, Alissa. You, Mr Mitchell and Mr Windsor will make your preparations and report in one hour to the docking bay. From there, you will go to these coordinates. You know the job from there, I assume.'

Alissa nodded.

'Good. Now get out of my sight.'

***

The docking bay on the Ark was quite a grand affair as it was used by many of the wealthy civilians to take little journeys around the Ark and its surrounding space. Garret, Underwood and Megan stood by a mini-ship that was barely the size of Alissa's living space. It would be big enough for the three of them, though they couldn't move about much, and it had a small area at the back for emergency medical treatment because Megan had insisted on it. She had told Alissa, 'If you do get in a fight, run. Get back to the shuttle and you can be treated from there. Don't be a hero.'

The three of them stood facing the captain as he gave them the final briefing for the mission.

'You are to board their ship and attempt to open a dialogue with their race. If this proves to be possible then as captain, I will open peace talks. Worst case scenario, it's every man for himself until we can rendezvous and try to find our way back.'

The three of then nodded to acknowledge their mission. Megan stepped forward next, 'Right, let me show you the emergency medical bay. Follow me.' She led them inside and to a bed along the back. She reached into a cupboard and pulled out a large plastic container.

'In here is everything you will need to save a life. Healing spray – Alissa, you've experienced this before – sedatives for any pain – you just put one end of the tube against your upper arm and press the button on the other end ... here. Then there are medications for poisons and antibodies for all known antigens.' She went through each item in the box carefully, ensuring they all understood how to use them.

'This information could save your life if they turn out to be hostile.'

'Thank you, Doctor.' Garret stepped inside the microship, which was beginning to feel crowded with five people. Megan climbed back out and left the captain with the others.

'Okay, time to go. Shem, Ham, vehicle checks please, external first.' The two of them nodded and followed in the direction that Megan had gone, leaving Alissa and Garret alone.

'You can save him if it doesn't jeopardise the safety of the Ark and her people.' With that he turned and walked out, leaving Alissa alone in the ship.

Vehicle checks only took an hour to fully complete on a ship so small, and by noon they were ready to depart and begin the mission. They were waved off, then suddenly they were in space. Shem was piloting the craft while Alissa and Ham carried out regular diagnostics. It would take them three hours to reach the coordinates. Short in comparison to the Ark's journey so far, but it felt like the last three hours of their lives.

'Guys.' Ham's voice cut through the silence. 'I'm scared.'

Shem and Alissa looked at each other, neither sure what to say. Finally Alissa responded: 'Me too, Ham.'

His eyes widened. 'You are?'

'Of course. We don't know what's going to happen. But we could be saving the lives of thousands of people. Isn't that worth it?'

'Yeah, I guess so.'

After the first hour one of the monitors in front of Shem bleeped. He glanced down and sighed. 'Well, that's it. We've dropped out of scanner range for the Ark.'

'We're alone,' Alissa said.

The silence returned. Alissa wanted to ease back into their relaxed chats but couldn't find the words. So instead they just sat, aware that they were speeding through space but unable to see a point of reference, something on which they could focus.

Towards the end of the second hour they saw something in the distance. A speck that grew as they closed in. Ham spotted it first.

'Hey, what's that dot?' He pointed into the distance. Shem tried to line up his gaze with Ham's arm.

'I dunno, man. Could be a planetoid, asteroid ...'

'A ship?' Alissa finished his thought.

Shem nodded. 'It's about the right distance but the scanners on this thing don't stretch that far.'

'I guess for now it's a mystery.' Alissa tried to smile and failed.

Halfway the through the third hour it became clear that it was not just a ship but a huge vessel, not dissimilar in size to the Ark herself.

'Wow ...' was all that Shem could manage.

Once they were within scanner range they began to analyse the configuration of the ship, and to identify sectors within it. Shem's panel was exploding with information.

'I've got multiple engines, weapons systems, a lot of life signs ...'

Then they were hailed. The three friends looked at each other. This was it, this was their moment. Alissa crossed her fingers just as her father had taught her as a child. She nodded to Shem to open the channel.

'Hello. My name is Alissa Namaah of the colony ship known as the Ark.'

They waited in silence until eventually the speaker crackled slightly then a voice came through, a deep voice that made them all feel uncomfortable.

'Greetings, humans. We observed your arrival in this sector and have been waiting for you. Please dock in the bay indicated on the plan being sent through to you now.'

Their panel bleeped and an image synthesis of the vessel flashed up on their screens. It showed the outer hull and numerous docking bays. One of them was lit up, and Shem could see a massive steel gate opening for them on the side of the ship.

The docking bay was considerably less grand than on the Ark. This was a working bay, filled with half-built ships and surrounded by steel walls, with grating for flooring. It reminded Alissa of the tech bays back in New Amerland but the thought didn't bring much comfort – she knew that somewhere in here there was an alien race, and she had to admit that a deep fear was growing within her.

The micro-ship gently touched down and Shem switched off the engines. The three of them sat in silence, waiting for what would happen next.

There was no movement in the docking bay; no sound. It was completely devoid of life. The three friends collectively held their breath in anticipation of what was to come.

While they waited, Shem scanned the internal atmosphere of the ship. The air was breathable to them, which was a relief to Alissa – it occurred to her that fighting their way out in space suits would have been impossible.

171

The hangar door whooshed open and three figures entered. The first thing that struck Alissa was how tall they were. They must've been over seven feet and were almost human in appearance, but for a pale blue tinge to their skin and a pronounced brow, not unlike the cavemen Alissa had seen in picture books as a child. There was, however, a slight reptilian feel to them. Alissa couldn't decide what it was about them – the shape of their mouths or their eyes – but something about them felt very wrong. They were of varying builds. The one in the centre had short black hair, wore long robes and had a slight paunch around his middle; the two on either side of him were bald, wore armour and held what Alissa could only assume were weapons.

Alissa reached out and took the hands of her best friends.

'I love you guys.'

None of them took their eyes off the three creatures.

Crossing the micro-ship in two steps, Alissa grabbed the locking mechanism on the door, a large wheel with spokes running through it, and turned it slowly. The door released and slowly raised up, revealing them to their alien counterparts.

The one in the middle spoke with a booming voice that demanded attention.

'Welcome to the Ik'Omeg, humans. The General has been expecting your arrival for some time now.'

'Wait, what? You speak our language?' It was struggle enough already to take in that aliens were standing in front of her. To have them turn out to be fluent English speakers was more that she was ready for.

'Of course.' The alien bowed his head slightly. 'We have observed your people for many centuries. Understanding the language makes that process much easier, I'm sure you'll agree.'

What came next looked like an attempt at a smile, but it came across as sinister. Alissa squeezed her companions' hands.

The alien who had spoken turned and started to walk out the door.

'Follow, please. But first, hand over your weapons.'

The guards with the guns motioned for Alissa, Ham and Shem to move towards them, and on unsteady legs, they did so.

Alissa carried two guns, and a knife for close-combat fighting. They were a security blanket for her and handing them over was at the bottom of her list of things to do on board an alien ship. Nevertheless, she felt she had to comply – they had come this far and there was no point in being gunned down in the hangar bay for refusing to cooperate. Following her lead, Ham and Shem handed over the small firearms they had each been assigned.

The alien in the robes smiled his sinister smile again. 'Excellent, my friends. Now come along. It's time to see the General.'

The interior of the ship was a fascination for Ham. They were guided through section after section of long steel-plated corridors. But the circuitry was visible. Full mechanisms were exposed on the walls, which meant that long wires ran alongside them as they walked. Some of them glowed that familiar blue hue he remembered from the hologram generator. Whatever power source they used seemed to have that one same side effect.

As they walked along the wide corridors, Ham examined the exposed workings as best he could. The ship reminded him a lot of the Ark in its basic structure. Perhaps there was a universal way to program something. He remembered something he had heard about the path of least resistance but couldn't quite make it fit what he was seeing, so he shrugged it off, wishing all the while that he still had some enhancement drugs left.

Alissa marched at the front, just behind the man in the robes. Her boots thudded against the steel-gridded flooring that reminded her bitterly of the Complex she had once lived in. It was a grim place to be, nothing like the Ark with its plush carpets and luxuries. The man in the robes looked out of place in these corridors, although the two armed guards fitted right in. Alissa's hand fell to her empty holster and she felt sick. Unarmed and out-numbered. Likely enough, this was only going to end one way for them. The only small relief was that they were being given a chance so speak to this General, whoever he may be, and Alissa intended to do everything in her power make peace with these creatures. But the pressure of knowing that the lives of every human currently living depended on her ability to smooth talk an alien made her suddenly light-headed.

They walked for what felt like a mile, up steel-gridded stairs and along exposed gantries and walkways, through more long corridors until they reached a door, outside which the robed man stopped.

'Ah, here we are then.' He pressed a button and with a mechanical whirr the door opened for them. He motioned for the three friends to enter the room.

Alissa walked in first. Unlike the rest of the ship, this room was grand in its design. Larger than the offices on the Ark, it was more or less square, with one wall of glass that curved outwards, allowing you to feel like you were reaching right out into space. The floor was covered in a spongy material of a beautiful deep red colour.

There was a desk in front of the windowed wall, behind which was a large, plush-looking chair with a high back. Alissa had never even seen material like it. The chair was turned away, facing the window. The walls were lined with shelves filled with books, ornaments and trinkets. The room was entirely the opposite of everything they had seen so far. It was tastefully decorated and lavish. Alissa hated it.

The robed man, who hadn't entered the room, smiled a grim smile and shut the door behind them.

Behind the desk, the chair slowly turned to reveal a creature with the same physicality as the other beings – the blue tinge to the skin, the pronounced brow and the reptilian feel – but this time clearly female. Her hair was long, with a deep purple shade which matched her eyes. Alissa felt exposed while this woman stared at her, unblinking and silent.

Eventually she rose to her feet and walked round the table to stand towering over Alissa, staring down at her. Defiant as ever, Alissa stared right back. This creature, Alissa was certain, was responsible for Silver Glove, for everything that had happened, and a wave of anger rushed over her. She wanted to hurt this 'woman'.

'Alissa. That's your name, isn't it?'

Her voice was soft, mesmerising. Alissa nodded dumbly.

'I'm so glad to have you here. Tell me, how far did you have to travel to meet us?'

Barely finding her voice, Alissa muttered, 'Too far.'

'Well, I'm sure you didn't travel all that way on that tiny ship of yours in the docking bay.'

Alissa didn't know how to respond to that, so held her silence. The woman's eyes narrowed as she continued: 'My name is Arley'Kiniere and I am the General.'

175

'Like the captain?' Hams voice jolted Alissa. The General's voice had a hypnotising quality and Alissa didn't trust that one bit.

'Yes, I'm like the captain of the ship.' Then she smiled. A long, sly smile. Alissa hated her.

'So, tell me Alissa, where is the Ark?'

'No.' Her voice was barely a whisper, but it wasn't easy to refuse a question from this creature.

'It's alright to be afraid, Alissa. Perhaps a friendly face will encourage you to be a little more open with us.'

The General pressed a panel on the desk and the door behind the three friends opened once more. In the doorway stood Silver Glove.

He walked towards the General, and Alissa stared open-mouthed. Since waking up on the Ark, Silver Glove had been nothing but a dream to her, and now here he was. For the first time in months she could smell his intoxicating scent and her eyes closed as she breathed him in.

'Alissa.' Shem hissed at her and her eyes flew open. Standing next to the General, Silver Glove smiled.

'I'm so glad you could be here, Alissa. It's been too long.'

She stepped forward and slightly to the side. She was manoeuvring herself in front of her friends, protecting them.

'What is this place?' Alissa kept her voice steady.

'It's a science vessel, Alissa. We take creatures from their home worlds and work to understand them. Dropping them back when they have served their purpose.'

'Why did you take me?' Alissa needed to know.

'That's enough for now, Alissa.' The General stepped forward. 'Tell us where the Ark is so we can take you back and discuss things further with your captain.'

176

'No. You'll never get to see it. All you want is to destroy it.'

The General began to lose some of her composure. 'You're not thinking clearly, human.' She almost spat the words out.

Alissa folded her arms and stood silently staring at the alien.

'You will, though, after some time.' The General glided across the room and pressed a few more buttons on her desk panel. 'You'll be escorted to the cells and held until I am ready to try again.' She turned to look directly at Alissa. 'You know from personal experience how skilled my men are at ... persuasion. I look forward to hearing your screams in person.'

The door whooshed open behind them and armed guards rushed in, grabbing the three prisoners by the arms and holding them tightly. Ham started to panic – Alissa could hear his grunts and cries as he was manhandled out. The sickening laughter of Silver Glove echoed around them while Shem was yelling at them to leave Ham alone. Through it all, Alissa continued to stare silently at the General as they dragged her away.

The cells were vile. They were half-dragged, half-carried through corridors until they reached a double door of solid steel. The guards used a handprint scanner to unlock the prison and dragged in their human cargo. This part of the ship was dark and dank. They had been taken down stairs and must've descended several floors. It smelled like the dead here. There were stains and scuffs all over the walls and floor. They reached a steel-studded wooden door with massive hinges. It swung open and the guards took the three into a large room with cells set into the walls and an archway at the back leading to more. Each cell had one or two occupants.

Some looked almost human but many looked completely alien to Alissa. Into one cell the guards tossed Ham and Alissa, slamming behind them a door made of steel bars and locked with a handprint scanner. Shem was dragged away, out of sight. Alissa called after him, praying he could hear her.

'I'll come for you, Shem. I promise.' She watched as Shem was dragged through the archway.

Alissa cursed and slammed her hand against the bars.

That's when she heard a soft weeping sound coming from behind her. She turned to see Ham curled up on the floor with his face buried in his arms. All the tension left her body as she watched him slowly rock himself to and fro while he cried, and she hated herself.

In seconds she had crossed the room, dropped to the floor and sat beside him. She gently stroked his back as he softly cried.

'It's okay. I'll get us out of here, Ham.' She didn't feel convinced and Ham could surely tell. Believing she was going to die on a mission was one thing, but being in the moment and facing the threat head-on was another matter entirely. For the first time she realised that Ham hadn't really understood just how dangerous and frightening this would be.

***

Shem had watched his friends being thrown into one cell while he was dragged further away.

'Hey, where are you taking me?' he shouted, struggling. 'ALISSA!'

He kept his eye on her until he was dragged through the archway away from them. There were more cells here, same as before, barred doors and forlorn-looking inmates. They walked to a cell with one prisoner inside, opened the door and tossed Shem inside. He landed on the steel floor, hitting his head hard. He swore as he tried to gather his thoughts, then he saw a pair of boots, right in front of him, and heard a familiar voice.

'Shem, are you okay?'

There are moments in life, he thought, where your blood runs cold and the hairs stand on end. Moments of pure fear. This was one of those moments. The voice was distinctive and unforgettable to him since the first time he heard it he was chained to a ceiling.

'Silver Glove.'

Shem rose slowly to his feet; he was barely able to maintain his composure. Soon they were face to face. Japheth looked at Shem with concern – there was blood slowly trickling from a gash on his head and he looked somehow angry and frightened at the same time. Japheth reached out a hand to try and guide Shem to the only chair in the cell, and Shem shrugged off the help, still not saying a word.

Japheth frowned. 'What did you call me? Silver Glove? That's not me, Shem.'

Just as the last words left his lips, a fist connected hard with Japheth's jaw, knocking him off balance. The fist was followed by Shem's shoulder ramming into Japheth's waist, sending him tumbling backwards to the ground. Crazed and fuelled by adrenaline, Shem landed hard on top of him and started raining punches at any part of Japheth he could reach, while the fallen man protected his head with his arms before eventually balling a fist, rolling onto his side and, with that momentum, punching Shem hard in the side of the head, knocking him sideways. Japheth pounced forward to try and pin

179

Shem to the ground. But he got a foot against Japheth's chest, kicking out hard and pushing him backwards into the cell door. Shem jumped up and ran at him, pinning him to the bars by his neck.

Shem didn't know how long he would have held Japheth there, cutting off his air supply. Maybe he would have killed him if left alone long enough. Instead, the door flew open, sending both men to the floor. One guard pulled the two apart and another two dragged the men to the back of the cell and shackled them beside each other to the wall.

Shem wasn't happy. His head was throbbing and he had a gash in his lip. Japheth was beginning to swell in the cheek and eye.

'Shem, I'm not Silver Glove.' He sounded exasperated.

'I know. She told me about you. About the dreams.'

Japheth let out a bitter laugh. 'So, you mangled my face out of jealously?'

'Shut up.' Shem stared hard at the floor.

'Absolutely not.' Japheth shuffled slightly. The manacles were uncomfortable and forced his arms into an awkward position above his shoulders. 'Look, I'm sorry. I fell in love with your girl. But in this place, you need something to keep you alive. To keep you sane. She did that for me.'

Shem scoffed in response, but Japheth carried on anyway.

'Our minds shared a connection, Shem. I met her through the hologram's eyes and I loved her strength and her heart. I saw her at her lowest moment, and I had the strength to be kind through the hologram. The man she calls Silver Glove is one of them, a creature called

180

Qatare. He controlled the hologram, Shem. But I was in there too. And I was fighting for her.'

Shem sat in silence; he honestly didn't know what to say and he was afraid his own confession of love for Alissa was mild and inconsequential in comparison. It made him feel bitter and defensive.

CHAPTER TWENTY-FOUR

THE GUARDS RETURNED TO ALISSA'S CELL AND opened the door cautiously, as if they were expecting a fight. But she didn't give them one. Alissa was still sitting beside Ham, rubbing his back and humming gently to him. When one of the guards stepped inside she was on her feet in an instant, like a mother defending her child, blocking the alien guard from coming any closer.

'You need to come with us now. The General wants to see you.'

His voice was authoritative and, looking behind him, Alissa saw four more armed guards. She didn't fancy her chances in an escape attempt.

'So, the General's told you to be a little more cautious around me?' Alissa stepped forward a little, and he stepped back uncomfortably. 'Good. She's right.'

It took considerable effort from Alissa not to punch the alien guard right in his face, but she decided that being gunned down was not something Ham needed to see.

Following the first guard and flanked by the other four, Alissa decided now was as good a time as any to find out what she could.

'Where's Shem?'

She was met with silence.

'I said, where is Shem?'

Still no one answered her, so she stopped dead in her tracks and folded her arms.

'Get moving, human.'

Now it was Alissa's turn to be silent. The guards raised their weapons.

'Get. Moving. Human.' Each word was said slowly, as if she didn't understand the language. 'Move, or we shoot you dead right here.'

Alissa looked at the guard who was speaking. Slowly, deliberately she responded:

'Since your General needs to know the location of my ship, I doubt she would allow you to shoot me. Tell me where my friend is, or we stand here for the foreseeable.'

She went back to staring straight ahead. The guards looked at each other until the one who had originally come to collect her spoke.

'He is in the holding cells with the other human. He has come to no harm.'

Alissa began moving forward once more to the General's office.

***

'I know you're not responsible for what happened to Alissa, or to me. But you've been in her head. You've done something to her.'

Shem's voice was unsteady, and he felt miserable.

'I owe you the truth. There's a device in my brain and it connects Alissa and me. Lets us share time together. In this place I needed that respite. I needed her.'

Shem sat silent for a moment. If it had been him – if he had been stuck here in this cell and had the chance to see Alissa every night – there was no doubt in his mind he would've taken it.

'Alissa was a moment of peace in a sea of torture. She was an angel sent to help me and I begged her for that help. I love her. But I'm not so dense that I believe she could ever love me back.'

Shem said nothing in response.

***

Ham was weeping silently into his arms, lying on the floor, unashamed in his emotion. He had been scared when Shem was taken away, and now Alissa was gone too. Maybe next they would take him, and he would end up dead. He manoeuvred into a sitting position and started picking at the metal flooring. A bundle of circuitry ran underneath the gridwork tiles, and he noticed a break in the wiring. It seemed strange to him, and he worked his fingers through the holes in the grating and pulled.

Ham has used all his strength to prise open the flooring panel. It was a tight fit but came loose eventually. The wiring was complicated and he could see why there was a gap. The wires ran into a darkened display screen. It would take a little forensic investigation but he believed that with time he could figure out how it worked.

***

Being hit in the face was an intense experience, especially with an open palm. The initial sting gave way to a dull burning pain that made her eyes water. Alissa did not care for it in the slightest, and gritted her teeth as another smack landed on her cheek.

'Tell me, Alissa. Where is your ship?'

The security chief tasted blood but was holding up well to the onslaught.

'I thought you said you were good at torture.'

The General paced the room in front of the chair and Alissa watched her movements. Eventually she turned back to Alissa and smiled.

'You will tell me. Your kind are known for being weak.'

'What do you know of my kind?' Her indignation was real. 'You stand here on this ship, deciding that humans should be wiped out, and for what? What did we ever do to hurt you?'

The General stopped pacing and pulled a chair closer to Alissa, sitting down to face her.

'Nothing has been done to affront me personally, but my orders come from the Committee and no one says no to them.' The General's voice was softer now. 'If the Committee wants you gone, your entire race will die.'

Alissa started to feel the bile rising in her throat, and the General continued: 'The Committee are responsible for your sun going supernova. They are responsible for the destruction of every Ark that has left Earth in the last decade.'

'Why?' was all Alissa could manage, and the General smiled.

'Your race has been monitored through its history by the Committee. As humanity expands it destroys its own world. You've ruined your own planet and now you wish to spread, like an infestation, throughout the universe? It will not be allowed.'

The General moved even closer, until her face was mere inches away from Alissa's.

'The incident that befell your planet fifty years ago was supposed to wipe you all out.'

'That's neither rational nor just.'

The General laughed. 'Life rarely is, Alissa.'

Alissa, her face still aching from the assault, frowned.

'You can't hold us responsible for something our ancestors did. Earth was doomed before I was even born. What this Committee is doing is genocide!'

The General cackled. 'Humans have committed genocide for centuries. The Committee watches over all the worlds and all the civilisations. They will not let humanity expand into the stars and destroy them.'

Alissa was no great wordsmith and her pleas were falling on deaf ears.

'So tell me, human. Now you understand, will you reveal to me the location of your ship?'

Alissa sat stern-faced and staring straight ahead.

'Alright, have it your way.'

The General walked round the desk to her chair and sat smiling in Alissa's direction as she pressed a few buttons on a panel. A voice emanated from a small speaker.

'Yes, General?'

'Bring me the fat one. Bring me Ham.'

CHAPTER TWENTY-FIVE

HAM HAD FINALLY MADE SENSE OF THE WIRING HE was looking at. A lot of the ship's systems were accessible through this screen and processor and it made sense to think that if there was an emergency it could be used to evacuate the prison. It had direct links to door locks within the prison, remote shuttle launchers and, most importantly to Ham, to a virtual transporter system. He started scanning the other cells for human life signs. He needed to find Shem. The system he was using was limited in scope – he could scan the cells, but not the whole ship.

It took a few minutes for the scanning to complete and when it did, it showed two humans sharing one cell, and while Ham thought Alissa had been taken away, it now looked more like she had been moved into another cell. A sigh of relief escaped his lips as he programmed the transporter to move the occupants of the two cells to another area of the ship. Only certain destinations would be available. The security office? Not likely. The ship's bridge? No way. The cargo hold ... That was the one. A vast open room filled with crates and containers to hide in. They could stay there until they figured a way out.

Ham made a few more keystrokes, hit Enter and suddenly felt light-headed. Everything went very bright and very blue. When the light dimmed again, he could see two men sitting on the floor next to where he was crouched. But the keyboard and screen weren't there anymore. He was in a new place. He was in the cargo hold.

Shem's voice distracted him from his awe at what he had just accomplished.

'Ham?'

Suddenly Shem's arms were round his shoulders.

'What happened? What did you do?'

Ham looked a little sheepish. 'I hacked into the ship's emergency systems.'

'That's brilliant, Ham. You did great.'

Ham smiled at the praise and Shem released his friend and stood back. That's when Ham noticed the other man standing with them.

'Wait, you're the guy from the transmitter! In Alissa's brain.'

Japheth took a step forward, hand extended. 'My name is Japheth. I'm a prisoner here and you just saved me.'

Ham took the hand cautiously and shook it, glancing at Shem, who was keeping a close eye on the man. Ham decided to keep an eye himself.

***

The General untied Alissa.

'You're free to return to your cell. I think perhaps your friend may be more talkative than someone like you.'

She gestured towards the door. 'Security are waiting outside to escort you.'

Alissa didn't move.

'Would you rather stay and watch what I have planned?'

Alissa balled her fists and took a few slow, precise steps towards the General. Then the comms pad buzzed on the desk. Without taking her eyes off Alissa the alien woman answered the call.

'Yes?'

A gruff voice replied: 'The humans. They've gone.'

'What?' The General turned to the comms pad and Alissa seized her chance.

Leaping forward she threw an arm around the General's throat, pulling her backwards towards the floor. Alissa wanted to lock her in a hold that would render the General unconscious but the alien woman wormed her long fingers between Alissa's arm and her neck, slowly prising herself free with remarkable strength.

Alissa grunted with effort as she tried to keep the hold but the General twisted free and swung a fist that connected hard. Alissa's cheekbone cracked as the punch landed and she yelped in pain. The General went to hit her again, but Alissa brought up an arm to block her and came back with a punch of her own that slammed into the alien's face, breaking the nose and spilling a deep purple blood. Alissa followed up with a kick to the mid-section. It hit the target, but the General was stronger than she appeared. She held onto Alissa's leg and swung her round, lifting her off the ground and tossing her into the bookcase beside them.

Falling to the spongy carpet and holding her ribs, Alissa groaned as the General stepped closer. The alien woman knelt behind Alissa and grabbed her by the hair, pulling her head back and lifting her front half off the ground. Another cry of pain came from Alissa. This was a fight she didn't want to have but if it gave her friends time to escape, then dying here at the General's hand would be worth it.

From behind, the General held Alissa's head in front of her own and wrapped her arms around her neck.

'I'm not sorry it ended like this for you. You're just a human. And when I'm done with you, I'm going to let your friends go and follow them right back to the last humans alive.'

Rage was all that Alissa felt. There was no way in hell she would let the General and her people follow the micro-ship back to the Ark. This had to end here. Alissa grabbed the General's head and pulled her forward, then, using her shoulder as leverage, she flipped the General over and onto the ground in front of her. Her fist balled once more, she pounded the General's face with all the anger she had left.

The alien lapsed into unconsciousness as Alissa stood over her prone body. The adrenaline rush was beginning to ease and now it was pain that was running through her nervous system, weakening her limbs until she fell against the shattered bookcase.

CHAPTER TWENTY-SIX

ALISSA WAS IN NEW AMERLAND, BACK IN SAIME'S Bar. In front of her was a glass of something that might once have been whisky. This didn't seem right. There was an alien, she was fighting ... Alissa closed her eyes and balled her hands into fists. Why wasn't she still fighting?

Am I dead?

It would make sense. The General had likely over-powered her and snapped her neck like a twig. This could be the afterlife. A tear fell and landed on her lap, followed by many more.

***

Shem started digging through boxes as Ham and Japheth kept watch. Eventually he found one labelled for the armoury. He broke open the seal and the box lid slid off to reveal six heavy weapons with shoulder straps. Shem and Japheth took one each while Ham stared at the rest.

'Hey Ham, leave the guns to us, okay?' Shem's voice was gentle and Ham nodded. He was relieved – there was no part of him that ever wanted to touch a gun. He really didn't want to hurt anyone. He wished again that he had saved some enhancers and he was annoyed with himself. He wanted to do *something* to help save them.

'We need to find Alissa.' As soon as the words left his lips Japheth smiled. 'I have an idea. But it could take a while and I don't really know if it'll work.'

Japheth sat on the floor, leaning against a crate, and closed his eyes. Ham and Shem both ducked down and waited in silence beside him.

Japheth reached out with his mind, the device in his brain amplifying his thoughts, spreading them until they reached their target. An unconscious Alissa.

***

The door to Saime's opened and Alissa glanced over. She had to look twice before she would allow herself to believe that it was Japheth. He crossed the room and pulled her to her feet, wrapping his arms around her.

'I'm so glad you're alive.'

'I may not be.' Her voice was quiet. 'I was fighting the General and ...'

'Alissa, you're alive. You must be, otherwise the device wouldn't work. But you're not conscious. You need to wake up. I'm with Ham and Shem in the cargo bay.'

Alissa barely dared to hope that this was real. 'They're safe?'

He nodded.

'Right, get them back to the hangar bay. I'll meet you there.'

192

'Alissa, be careful.' He leaned in and kissed her. 'Sorry. That might be my last chance.'

The world faded around her as Alissa opened her eyes to the pain and carnage of the waking land.

She climbed to her feet and began to search the office. She found two beautifully ornate handguns in the General's desk. Carefully she stepped towards the door and took a few deep breaths; she needed to block out the pain for a little longer, to get her friends out safely. With a gun in each hand, she used the butt of one to open the door, and then held them both in front of her. No guards turned to look so she took a step out, pointing the guns sideways with outstretched arms. Each of them was pressed into the face of a guard, and she pulled the trigger without even considering what she was doing. It was only as their bodies thudded to the ground that she took a moment to realise she had killed them.

**

While Japheth was coming back to reality, Ham stared off into space. But he wasn't imagining lovely things. He was running through the scenarios in his head, imagining all the ways things could go wrong. Then his eyes lit up.

'I need to go to Engineering!'

Shem and Japheth looked at him, then at each other. Shem took a step towards him.

'That's not gonna be an easy task; there will be a lot of crew between us and the engines.'

Ham looked down. 'If we leave, they'll follow us. We have to go to Engineering.'

'Okay. We'll try.'

193

The long, steel corridors stretched on before the three men as they ran towards their goal. The location of the engine room was easily established using a nearby wall panel. Once they knew where to go, it was just a case of getting there. They were taking corners at speed when they came across a group of crewmen working on some wiring, blocking the corridor completely. There was a moment of confusion as the tall, alien creatures stared at the armed humans, before the realisation hit. One of the aliens reached for a weapon as another reached to sound an alarm; both were dead within seconds, causing the other three to flee in fear. Shem and Japheth shot them in the back.

There was quiet in the corridor for a moment. Ham was crying silent tears; Shem was leaning against the wall with his head in his hands and Japheth was keeping watch. Swallowing big gulps of air, Shem tried to keep himself from vomiting. They had just been crewmen doing their jobs, and there would be more between them and safety.

'I can't do this.'

Shem's voice was breathy and shaking, but Japheth's was the cold voice of reason.

'Unfortunately, Shem, you have to. Or we all die, including Alissa.'

'That's not fair.'

'I suppose it isn't, but nevertheless it's true.'

Shem pulled himself up straight, his hands on his gun, and set his face in a stony expression.

'Alright, let's keep going.'

He hoped he came across to the others as believable, but on the inside Shem was shaking. Japheth took the lead and Ham walked in the middle of the group. They were moving slower now, desperately hoping not to run into more aliens.

The corridors were empty and Shem began to wonder what time it was on this ship, and whether they were running on a skeleton crew. He asked Japheth.

'I don't know, to be honest. They don't really discuss the schedule with prisoners.'

It made sense but didn't stop Shem wondering.

They had almost made it to Engineering undetected when a shrill alarm sounded. It was very probable that someone had happened across their earlier massacre and raised the alarm. Now the real fight would begin.

Shem and Japheth raised their guns as they walked, ready to fire at a moment's notice. A security detail came running around a corner. Japheth reacted first and shoved Ham back and into an adjacent hallway, away from the gunfire, following him in to use the wall as a shield. Shem threw himself into one of the inset doorways, just barely making it without a bullet ripping through his flesh.

When the firing stopped for a moment, both men leaned out and shot at the security detail. The aliens had left themselves exposed by approaching so far. Shem and Japheth took them down easily enough, and when they were fallen they took their weapons.

Engineering was only a few metres away. They ran in and Ham immediately went to the console he needed, as though he knew the place. Shem and Japheth took defensive positions and kept watch. The place was deserted, probably evacuated because of the alarm.

As security men came in, they were picked off one by one. It was all looking too easy, until Shem got himself shot. It was a strange sensation; he didn't feel anything at first, then his shoulder was suddenly warmer than the rest of him. He looked down and saw the deep red soaking into his uniform. Then the pain came.

He cried out and stumbled backwards. Japheth tried to cover Ham alone but they were getting overwhelmed.

'Shem!' he called out. 'Can you keep going?'

Lifting the gun was agonising but Shem did his best. After a few more moments Ham finally spoke: 'It's ready. We need to go now.'

The three men looked at each other and then took off for the hangar bay at a full sprint.

***

Alissa had slipped silently past a few guards and crewmen and was beginning to feel quietly confident about her escape. Then she turned the corner to find two guards blocking her path. They were both armed and raised their guns to shoot. Alissa's instinct kicked in before her brain and before she knew it she had dodged their opening blasts and without hesitation, she fired twice, hitting each guard between the eyes. It should've been painful for her, but this was what she was trained for – this was what Silver Glove had done to her. She could detach from the violence, at least for the time being, which was all she needed.

The hangar bay doors were guarded, and an alarm had sounded a few minutes earlier. They would be expecting an escape attempt, but it looked like heavy security hadn't reached the hangar yet. Alissa shot three of the guards with deadly accuracy. As they fell to the ground she charged in, subjecting a fourth to a flurry of blows that sent him flying to the ground, and kicking a fifth guard behind her just enough to knock him off balance. She turned to shoot him, but both guns clicked impotently.

She lunged for the guard's gun as he brought it up and they fought for it, Alissa barely managing to wrest it from his grasp and use it to shoot him and the remaining guard.

This was her chance to breathe, just for a moment, to take a brief respite. Her ribs were agony and her the rest of her wasn't holding very well either. Her head throbbed and she prayed that would be the end of it. Then she was tackled from behind.

A very angry, bloody General pinned Alissa to the ground and rained savage blows down on her, pulverising the right side of her ribs and using her clawed fingers to tear into the skin of her arms as Alissa protected her face. The finesse of their first fight was gone – this was a brutal and visceral attack, born of rage.

Suddenly the attack stopped. Alissa could still feel the weight of the General pinning her to the ground, and gritting her teeth she moved her arms slightly away from her face, just to see what the alien was doing. The creature had pulled out a long and jagged knife and slowly lifted it above Alissa's chest.

There was a part of Alissa that was desperately trying to move, to shake her off and fight back, but every movement was excruciating; there was nothing left but pain and she just prayed that it would be quick. She wanted to close her eyes, but couldn't look away from the General's crazed face.

The next few moments happened in slow motion. The General raised the blade high above her own head, and it hung there for just a moment. As she started to bring the blade down something connected with the side of her head, knocking her completely off balance. It was the butt of a gun. Someone had hit the General hard enough to send her sideways across the floor. Then that someone picked up the blade and drove it hard into the General's chest, causing great gouts of dark purple blood to pour onto the floor between them.

Strong arms gently lifted Alissa and cradled her to a firm chest, and Alissa, with all she had left, raised her head to see what was happening. The last face she saw before she slipped out of consciousness was Shem's.

CHAPTER TWENTY-SEVEN

SHEM HAD BEEN THE FIRST OF THE THREE TO round the corner and the scene before him caused him to stop in his tracks. There were guards, dead and bleeding, on the metal floor, and the General was sitting on a prone figure, holding a serrated blade high in the air. Without thinking Shem had raised his gun and pulled the trigger. The gun gave a hollow click and Shem growled angrily. And in the next instant he charged into the fight.

He had barely been aware of the voice behind him shouting for him to be careful; he ignored every sound until, using all his might, he slammed the butt of the gun violently into the temple of the General. Then, still on auto pilot, he had grabbed the knife and driven it into the alien's chest. Just to make sure.

Once he had dispatched the General he turned his attention to Alissa. She was in a bad state. As gently as he could, he picked her up and held her close to his chest, smiling down at her as she fell out of the waking world.

'Shem.'

It was Japheth.

'Shem, give her to me, you're losing a lot of blood. You were shot, remember?'

Shem just shook his head. 'No. I'll take her.'

They reached the micro-ship and climbed on board. Shem laid Alissa on the bed at the back and Japheth immediately started working on her wounds, using the healing spray to repair the damaged flesh. The sensor he passed over her body showed a number of broken bones and he had no way of fully repairing them. While her skin was slowly knitting together, Shem got the engine started and the ship slowly rose up off the gantry. Ham was frantically hitting buttons on the panel in front of him.

'Ham, we need the doors open, buddy.' Shem's voice was calm in its urgency.

The doors leading back into the body of the ship opened once more and guards started to pour in.

'Ham, the doors.'

Shem's voice grew louder. His shoulder was still bleeding from the gunshot and he was starting to feel dizzy. He had to get the ship out of here, now.

'Ham! The doors!'

As he spoke, the doors started to open, and he went to maximum power and launched them out of the hangar and into the blackness of space at great speed.

A few seconds later, Japheth was at his side, pressing a white gauze against the bullet hole to stop the bleeding and injecting something into his neck.

'What are you doing?'

'I can't use the healing spray; it's agonising and you'll lose control of the ship. I've given you adrenaline – it should keep you going until we get far enough away.'

With gritted teeth, Shem nodded and concentrated on steering the micro-ship. Suddenly, the whole craft shook, sending Japheth tumbling to the ground. He crawled back over to the bed and strapped Alissa down as the ship shook once more.

Shem yelled: 'What the hell is going on?'

Ham was scanning as best he could to see if they were under attack, when the screen in front of him beeped and showed him an image of the science vessel. It wasn't heavily armed but it had enough gun turrets to cause the micro-ship some problems.

Shem was engaging in some incredible evasive manoeuvres, sending Japheth, the only person not strapped into anything, flying around the back of the ship. He hung onto a metal bulkhead and closed his eyes, as though in prayer.

Then Ham's visual vanished in an orange light and a sea of tiny pieces. The vessel had exploded behind them. The shockwave hit the micro-ship and Shem gritted his teeth as he tried desperately to control their trajectory. It took a while, but the ship evened out. Once they had reached a steady speed, Shem turned to Ham.

'Did you ... Is that what you did, in the engine room?'

Ham hung his head. 'I'm sorry Shem, I was scared they'd follow us. I had to stop them.'

'You did stop them, buddy. We're safe. The Ark is safe.'

***

After an hour, Alissa started to stir, then groaned as she opened her eyes. Japheth was beside her, holding her hand as she came round.

201

'Am I dreaming again?' she asked as his face came into focus.

He laughed gently. 'No, you're awake.'

Bone crunched against bone as she tried to sit up and she cried out in pain.

'I'm sorry, Alissa. There's nothing more I can do to help until we get back to your ship.'

Lying back down, Alissa thought about the General.

'They'll be chasing us. We're gonna lead them straight back to the Ark.'

'No, we won't.' Japheth looked over at Ham. 'Their ship was destroyed. We're safe.'

Alissa remembered what the General had said about the Committee, how she was working for them.

'They'll be back. It's not over.'

She groaned in pain as she turned her head to look at the back of Ham and Shem's chairs. She had expected all of them to die in that place. Blinking back tears, she tried to rest for the journey back.

CHAPTER TWENTY-EIGHT

THE HANGAR BAY DOORS OPENED, ALLOWING THE micro-ship to land safely on board the Ark. Garret had felt sick – the feeling of guilt had been deepening for the last eighteen hours. The longer the away team had maintained radio silence, the more he had worried that he would never see them again.

There had also been that glimmer of hope that maybe they could initiate peace talks. Maybe they would come back with a member of the alien crew, ready to talk about the future of humanity within the vast universe. He didn't know what to think when the micro-ship reappeared on the scanner, with burn marks on the hull and damage to the rear.

Running through the ship wasn't something he often did at his age, but he ran today. He was desperate to get to the hangar and see how many had survived. The doors slid open for him and he ran in to find Underwood and Megan already there, opening the micro-ship doors to release the away team.

Shem emerged first, much to Megan's dismay when she saw his shoulder. She checked the wound and ordered him straight to the infirmary. Ham was next, uninjured but shaken, and Garret ordered him to join Shem in the infirmary.

Next out was Japheth, pulling behind him the small medibed on which Alissa was strapped.

'Oh my God.' The words tumbled out before Megan could stop them.

'Do I look that bad?'

'I need to get you to the infirmary, now! Ham, can you push the bed?' Ham nodded and grasped the bar at the head end.

Japheth watched as his saviours left, leaving him alone with the captain of this ship and another officer. He nodded respectfully but with an awkwardness that Silver Glove never showed.

'You are Japheth, I presume?'

He nodded again.

'Alright then. I appreciate you're not an officer here, but I would like you to accompany me to my office for debriefing.'

'Of course; I'll do whatever I can to help.'

'Thank you.' Garret turned and began walking across the hangar bay. Japheth followed with Underwood close behind him, a stern look etched onto her face.

***

'Will someone please explain what happened out there?'

Megan was standing beside Alissa's bed, waving a large paddle over her torso, healing the broken bones.

204

Alissa's face had been healed first but her body was taking longer. Megan had given her something for the pain.

One of the other doctors, an older man with a bald head whose name no one could quite remember, was knitting the wound on Shem's shoulder with a small pen-like device that he was passing to and fro. It emitted an energy that encouraged painless and rapid cell regeneration.

Megan was satisfied that Ham hadn't been physically hurt in the fight, but she worried for his mental condition since he was sitting in silence, staring at them.

'They threw us in a cell. Ham got us out. We even saved Japheth.' Shem still couldn't quite say his name without grinding his teeth. Megan raised an eyebrow and looked down at Alissa.

'Japheth? As in ...'

'Silver Glove.' Alissa finished the sentence for her. 'And I had a bit of a fight with the ship's captain, who they call the General.'

'A bit?' Megan was incredulous. 'You look like you were run over by a subway car!'

'Okay, a big fight.' Alissa shifted on the bed slightly. 'But if you think this is bad, you should see the General.'

'Where is the General?' Megan asked, not knowing if she actually wanted the answer.

'Dead.' The reply came from Shem. 'They're all dead.'

'Oh.' The room fell silent while Megan continued to work on Alissa. The doctor fixing Shem's shoulder left, but Shem and Ham both stayed back, waiting for   Alissa.

***

'Please, take a seat.'

Garret motioned to the chair facing his desk and Japheth sat down.

'As I'm sure you can imagine, we have only known about you from Alissa's descriptions. Which haven't always been glowing.'

Japheth looked down at his hands while Garret continued: 'What do you know of Alissa's experiences back in New Amerland and then here on board the Ark?'

'It was like watching it through someone else's eyes. I could see and feel everything he did, but I had no control over it. I couldn't stop him.' He knotted his fingers together. 'Sometimes, he would slip. Loosen his grip on me and I could … I could try and make sure she was coping. With what they were doing.'

Garret listened carefully as Japheth spoke, but something Alissa told him was troubling him.

'There were four of you that took her. What happened to the other three humans?'

'I don't know. I've never seen them outside of the projection. I couldn't tell you whether they were on that ship or not.'

'What about the aliens who controlled the actions of the holograms?'

'Silver Glove, or whoever he was, was on the ship. We were both strapped into a machine to be combined into the image that Alissa saw.'

Garret continued to question Japheth, going back to when they first took him, how they treated him, where he was put on the ship, how many aliens interacted with him and many more questions in a similar vein. It went on for well over an hour before Garret finally said:

'Alright, Japheth. You are as much a victim in this as Alissa. You're no prisoner here and you're free to go. I'll organise civilian quarters for you. However, I do want

Megan to organise a brain scan and removal of your tracker.'

Garret stood and held out a hand to Japheth.

'Welcome to the Ark.
'

***

Alissa jumped off the gurney and hopped on the spot a couple of times.

'I feel great, Megan!' She hugged the pregnant doctor. 'We'd better get to Garret and explain what happened over there.'

As they left the infirmary they happened upon Japheth and one of Alissa's officers coming their way. Here she was, sound of mind and body. Fully conscious and standing right in front of Silver Glove. But the real man, flesh and blood. They stood in front of each other for a moment, unmoving. Shem and Ham hung back a little.

Alissa raised a hand and gently touched his cheek. 'You're real.'

He covered her hand with his own. 'Yeah, I suppose I am.' She smiled awkwardly at him, then the realisation hit that they weren't alone in their own world. She withdrew her hand while Japheth returned her awkward smile with one full of warmth.

'Thank you, Alissa. You saved my life.'

'I ... You're welcome.' Speaking to him in the flesh was such a new experience for her. He had Silver Glove's face, but he wasn't him. The confidence and the intensity were all gone. He was just a man, like all other men.

'Sir, I need to get this man to the infirmary.' The security officer stepped forward slightly.

'Of course! I'm sorry, go right ahead.'

207

Alissa, along with Ham and Shem, stepped aside to allow Japheth to pass and continued along the corridors of the Ark.

'Noah, is the captain still in his office?'

'No, Alissa. The captain is currently on the bridge.'

She looked at the others and shrugged her shoulders. 'Bridge it is, then.'

The three friends turned down the next corridor and started towards the ship's transit system.

***

Garret stood on the bridge with Underwood, looking out into space. He needed the ship back on its original course, to get the crew back into their routines, then he would focus on Alissa, Ham and Shem and what had happened out there.

'Okay, let's get this boat back in the water.'

Underwood gave him a sideways glance. It was something Captain Andover used to say, and she realised then how much she missed him.

Garret was a good captain, but he was different to Clarke. Less relaxed, more stern. But over time, he'd grow into the job and she looked forward to that day.

'Aye aye, skipper,' came the response from the nav officer, who relayed the message to the nav deck and gave the bearings. They would steer the colossal ship in the direction requested. Except that when the ship began to pick up speed, it suddenly juddered. Just a small ship quake but enough to grab the attention of those on the bridge.

'What the hell was that?' Garret turned to his security officer, who was tapping on his control panel and frowning. 'Sir, there are seven small vessels surrounding us. They appear to be firing on us.'

'Well, get us out of here. Fast!'

The nav officer sent the command for full speed and the ship did start to increase its velocity.

'Sir.' It was the first officer. 'Their weapons are weakening what's left of our shield.' Alice turned to Garret as the ship started to shake more violently. 'Captain, they're gonna break through that shield and we can't outrun them with only one engine.'

'So ... what, Alice? What are you saying?'

'I'm saying that we need to evacuate the ship, Garret. Before it's too late.'

Garret hesitated only for a second. He sent the bridge crew to the 'lifeboats': small escape pods built for one or two people, and prayed the ship would hold long enough to evacuate the crew.

***

Ham, Shem and Alissa were on their way to the bridge when the first shock hit. There was a moment of confusion, then the ship shook again. Alissa's stomach sank at the memory of Andover dying in the explosion. That was how the ship felt then.

Ham said, 'What the hell's going on?' He sounded scared and Alissa's response wasn't reassuring.

'I don't know.'

With one hand she took hold of Ham's arm, and with the other motioned for Shem to follow her. They started to jog back the way they had come. There were a great number of stairways to negotiate in order to reach other decks, and Alissa was leading them to one when N.O.A.H. announced a ship-wide message from the captain:

'All hands, it is with regret that I order you to abandon this ship with immediate effect.'

Then the alarm sounded.

***

Under a gurney, Megan had one arm around her stomach and the other pushing against the underside of the bed, holding herself in place. But it was a struggle. The ship around her was lurching violently and Megan lost her grip, spilling out onto the floor. She felt a snap and her arm exploded in pain as it broke beneath her. Crying out, she held her good arm tight to her bump while the broken arm spread limply along the floor as she curled into the foetal position.

Japheth was beside her in an instant, picking her up and moving her back to the gurney. He placed her underneath is as gently as he could. He crouched in front of her, holding the bed down and using his body to protect her. Bottles were falling as the ship bucked and juddered around them, and the rest of the medical staff found what shelter they could as the shaking worsened.

***

Alissa was running through corridors with Ham and Shem at her heels. They helped people as best they could, sending them towards the lifeboats as the ship bucked beneath their feet. People were falling and being trampled underfoot. It reminded Alissa, in a sick way, of New Amerland. It was surprising how quickly people fell back into self-preservation mode. In an emergency it was easy to spot those who grew up in a place like New Amerland. They were more selfish, more obsessed with saving themselves. Alissa stopped to help a woman to her feet after three men had charged past her, knocking her to the floor.

***

After the announcement to evacuate, the medical staff emerged and ran for the doors. Sahline stopped by the gurney.

'Megan, we have to go.' Sahline held out her hand but Megan stayed where she was. 'I can't, it's too dangerous out there.' As if to prove her point, the ship violently shook again. Sahline looked to the door, then back at Megan. Japheth chimed in: 'Megan, if you want to evacuate, I'll help you.'

'This is the infirmary; it's designed to withstand a lot of impact. If I was going to be on a ship that's going down, this is the room I'd choose. And since I am, I have.'

Japheth nodded and turned to Sahline. 'You can stay with us, you don't have to run.'

She shook her head. 'I'm sorry,' she said, and bolted for the door.

Japheth turned back to Megan. 'I wish there was something I could do.'

'You're doing plenty. I promise.'

***

Garret was watching the scanners. The Ark was surrounded by small attack vessels, all of which were firing on them. There was nothing he could do except watch his ship crumble around him. His mind drifted to Clarke.

Would this have happened if he were still alive? Would he have allowed Alissa to meet with the aliens? It was doubtful – Clarke would've seen another way out, another choice.

This is my fault, he told himself. The people who die today, die because of me.

At that moment, the power failed and Garret was plunged into darkness.

At the same moment Garret and Underwood braced themselves on the bridge, Megan was screaming from under a gurney as Japheth took her hand, and Alissa was spread-eagled in a hallway having fallen head first in the darkness. Alissa turned and saw the shadowy outline of a body curled up. In the darkness she reached out, felt the neck. There was no pulse. Ham and Shem arrived seconds behind her and almost fell over her. They crouched beside their friend.

'Alissa. Is he okay?' Shem's voice was shaking.

'No. He's dead.' She rose to her feet. 'We need to keep moving. It's not far to the boats.'

Within a few minutes of the power cutting out completely, the emergency lights clicked on. They were just about bright enough for people to move safely through the corridors. Alissa charged ahead while Shem and Ham tried to keep up, and as she turned the corner to the evac station she saw that there was just one escape pod left.

The first thing that struck Alissa was how small the pods really were. Three wouldn't fit; two would struggle if one of them was Ham. Shem arrived seconds later followed by Ham.

'Okay Ham, in you go.' Shem reached past him and pulled the lever to open the door. Ham climbed inside and shuffled slightly in the seat.

Alissa turned to Shem. 'I need you to take care of Ham,' she said. 'You're next.'

He nodded but turned quickly, shoving Alissa into the pod and pulling the lever almost simultaneously. Alissa stumbled and fell onto Ham, pushed herself up and pressed against the glass as the escape pod fell from the Ark.

***

There was a deafening crunch as the ship started to break apart. Shem stayed to watch the pod fall as long as he could, but the cold had started creeping into the bay. He had to find a way to hide. He turned to run as the floor disappeared from beneath his feet.

***

Alissa was still pressed against the window of the pod, watching Shem shrink as the ship grew more distant. In moments they had drifted so far from the Ark that she could see the whole ship. She stared open-mouthed as the ship that she had fought so hard to get onto, the ship that had become her home, broke apart.

Fighter ships were swirling around them, chasing pods and picking them off. All they could do was fall towards the ringed planet and hope.

The sights that came next for Alissa were some of the most horrific she had ever experienced. There were people being blown out of the ship and floating through space with no protection, their faces bloated and frozen in silent screams. The Ark had split apart into huge sections which were caught in the same gravity as their pod. They watched as the fragments fell alongside them

213

for a few moments, then disappeared through the clouds beneath them. Alissa cried as she watched the fighter ships attack escape pods one by one, blowing them into nothingness.

Alissa and Ham hugged as their pod's emergency thrusters kicked in and gently lowered them to the ringed planet's surface amid the carnage and twisted metal; and with a tear-streaked face, Alissa pressed some of the buttons by her seat and waited for N.O.A.H.'s response. All she got was a readout, because there was no N.O.A.H. anymore, there was nothing for the pod to connect to, it was running off its own database now.

Ham let out a pained cry. 'Alissa,' he said, barely getting the words out, 'is Shem dead?'

Alissa stared at the readout in her hand, tears falling freely from her eyes onto the paper.

'I don't know, Ham.'

The readout simply advised that the air was light but breathable, and that there were no detectable toxins and no immediate threats to human life.

'We have to go out there Ham. Any other pods need to be found and survivors counted.'

He nodded and tried to stifle his tears. 'Will there be more dead people out there?'

Alissa wrapped her arms around Ham.

'Yes, I think there will be.'

Ham started to cry again, and Alissa gently shushed him.

'Ham, there will be people out there who need us.'

She opened the door of the pod and stepped outside. The sky above was grey, but with a tinge of orange from the burning wreckage that spread out across the landscape.

214

The largest part of the Ark was just a few hundred metres away. The ship was a massive feat of technological advancement for mankind and, as such, there was a lot of it. She stood for a minute to take it all in. Her home, her job and her life were all on that ship. Now it was burning across an alien world and while the sound of a hundred roaring fires was deafening, it didn't drown out the cries and screams of the people with whom she had shared this home.

'HAM!' Alissa screamed his name. 'Help me. There are people in the wreckage who are alive!'

The look of horror on Ham's face was one she hoped never to see again, and the two of them ran to the wreckage, clambered through a gaping hole in the shattered hull and started running through broken rooms and corridors. They heard the cries of a woman coming from what looked like a chunk of the civilian quarters. Lifting steel sheeting, charred furniture and even chunks of carpeted flooring, Alissa and Ham found a badly burned woman begging for help. They pulled her free but by the time they had reached the dusty terrain of the planet she had fallen unconscious.

'Ham we need to find a medic. Someone to help these people.'

'Okay, Alissa. I'll do whatever you say.'

'So, let's find what's left of the infirmary and get supplies and hopefully a doctor.' She didn't dare to mention but she prayed she would find Megan safe and well.

While they searched, Alissa found her fair share of people who hadn't been as lucky as her, and with each corpse, the hope of ever finding Shem dwindled.

After an hour of searching, they had pulled many people, both living and dead, from the wreckage. Then Alissa spotted a section of corridor she recognised. It was hanging out the side of a large portion of the ship that had stayed quite intact. It led to the infirmary. Leaving Ham, Alissa ran to it and jumped to grab the edge of the floor. The corridor hung diagonally, and it took a lot of effort to pull herself up and onto the singed carpet. On her hand and knees, she steadily climbed towards the infirmary.

In two hundred metres she turned off the corridor and into the next one. To catch her breath, she leaned against the wall for a few moments. The ship groaned and creaked around her. It wouldn't last – sooner or later it was going to fall to pieces and anyone they didn't rescue would be lost. She pushed on until she reached the infirmary doors. With no power, they had to be opened the old-fashioned way.

With a grunt, Alissa pulled one of the doors sideways. It was slow going, but she managed to get her foot into the gap. She set her back against the door and pushed until it clicked and locked into place, leaving enough space to pass through.

Scanning the room, Alissa spotted the medicine cabinet and clamoured over to it. The room was at an angle and most of the furniture had crashed against the wall. She grabbed a medical bag, opened it and laid it down under the cabinet doors. They were locked, so hopefully the contents were safe. Alissa yanked on the padlock, ripping it off the doors and pulling them open. Pen injectors fell from the shelves into the open bag and Alissa moved to the next cabinet. By the time she had finished, she had piled up four bags of meds and tools.

'Now all I need is a doctor.'

She laughed bitterly as she passed the straps over her shoulders.

As she made her way slowly back to the doors, she heard a groan escape from underneath a gurney that was jammed against the wall with the rest of the furniture. Alissa froze. She knew what she had heard – there was someone trapped in there.

'I'm here,' she shouted. 'I'm gonna help you.'

Alissa pulled chairs, tables and gurneys away until she saw Megan, curled up in a ball somewhat protected by mattresses from the infirmary.

'Megan?'

The doctor looked up, shaking and sobbing.

'What happened?' She just about managed to get the words out and through her own tears Alissa managed to explain.

'It was them, the aliens. They attacked the Ark, they destroyed it. We landed on the ringed planet.'

Megan held her bump protectively. 'He's moving around a lot. I think he's okay.'

Alissa looked back to the door.

'I have to get back out there, Megan, I have to keep searching.' She looked down at the doctor. 'It's gonna be hard, but we need to get you out to the surface. It's not safe in here.'

Megan nodded, then her eyes widened. 'Japheth was here! He was protecting me.' She started looking around. 'Alissa, where did he go? Is he okay?'

Alissa stared at Megan. 'I haven't seen him.'

The women started calling his name as Alissa hauled more furniture away from the wall, searching for the man who had appeared to her so many times in her dreams. *He can't be dead*. There was too much that Alissa still needed to know. So many questions whirling in her mind. He wasn't *allowed* to go anywhere until she had answers.

217

Pulling back a steel cabinet she found him, against the wall, his face broken and bleeding.

'Megan! Help me ...'

Seconds later the doctor was by her side, her shattered arm strapped to her side, rooting through the medical bags that were still hanging from Alissa's shoulder. She grabbed a small scanner and passed it over Japheth several times.

'He's pretty banged up, Alissa. Three broken bones, a small puncture in his lung and a hefty concussion.'

Megan began to administer drugs to the semi-conscious man while Alissa made her way slowly back to the door. Looking out, she called back to Megan: 'Look, I need to get you two out of here. The Ark fell from space, there's no telling how delicate this whole thing is.'

As in, one wrong move and it might just come crashing down around us.

Megan continued to treat Japheth while Alissa scoured the infirmary one more time. She managed to pack another two duffel bags with equipment and drugs, and found a cupboard containing bed straps. With raised eyebrows she showed them to Megan.

'They're for strapping in difficult or dangerous patients, Alissa.'

'Could they be used to transport an unconscious person through a broken ship?'

Megan nodded. 'Alissa, you're a genius.'

'I often think so.'

While Megan stabilised her patient, Alissa started work on linking the straps together and attaching them to a steel rail beside the doors. If the rig held, they would be able to lower Japheth to the far side of the twisted corridor.

Alissa made three loops, one for each of his legs and one to pass round his chest and shoulders. When he was securely attached, Alissa tied a long length of webbing onto one of the loops, manoeuvred him to the doorway and lowered him out, gently delivering him to the far side of the corridor.

'Okay. Are you sure you're up to this, Megan?'

'Only one way to find out.' The doctor swung herself down using her good arm, took hold of the straps and started pulling Japheth towards the turning in the corridor.

Alissa fed the webbing over her shoulder, using the steel rail as a brake. It was easy going until Megan called out that she was pushing Japheth over the edge.

Alissa's muscles burned as she held his weight, slowly lowering him as best she could. It took several long minutes to get Japheth to the ground. Alissa followed, helping Megan to negotiate the last drop to the ground. Finally, she dropped into a sitting position beside Japheth, looking up at the massive bulk of their ship.

'There could be people in there. Trapped and dying. But I can't save them all.'

Ham seemed to come out of nowhere, followed by three bruised and battered looking civilians.

'We can help.'

It was agreed that the three civilians would continue to search, and bring any injured parties back to Megan for treatment. Using the medical supplies they had recovered, the doctor started to set up a makeshift infirmary.

***

Over half a mile away from where Alissa had searched, Shem crawled out from under the wreckage. Burnt faux leather and steel sheeting surrounded him as he pulled himself free. There was silence around him but for the crackling of flame and his own heavy breathing. The Rec had ended up being the closest place to him when the ship started going down, so he had hidden himself under a table in there and thought about Alissa.

Shakily, he rose to his feet, wincing at a gash on his thigh. Blood had soaked into his trouser leg and immediately he felt woozy. He grabbed a piece of the upholstery and tied it over the wound, hoping that it would be enough to stem the bleeding until he could find help. He had assumed the Rec had survived the crash but when he took a minute to take in his surroundings he saw that half the Facility was missing. Limping to the edge of the floor, he realised he was two floors up, looking out over a landscape of burnt and twisted steel.

Shem's voice didn't carry any great distance as he called out, the groaning of hot steel as it cooled drowning him out with its own death cry. He started to make his way through the wreckage. At one point he pulled away some debris to reveal the corpse of Ryan. It felt like a thousand years since their fight. Shem choked back tears as he respectfully covered the half-burnt body and sat beside it. There were no voices, no one moving through the chunks of alloy and steel.

Shem was alone.

He sat for a long time, his head resting in his hands, shoulders shaking as he wept. Until a hand gently tapped his shoulder. Shem leapt to his feet and whirled round. Standing in front of him was a short woman in late middle age, wearing civilian clothes. She gave him a half-smile,

'Are you hurt?'

Shem shook his head. 'No, I'm fine.'

The woman glanced down at his bloodstained pants leg and her eyes narrowed. 'You need medical attention. If that gets infected, you'll die.'

Shem dropped an arm to cover the staining as best he could. 'Are you alone?'

The woman smiled. 'There's a few survivors just over the ledge. I came up here to see if I could spot where the infirmary landed. We need medical supplies.'

'Are you a doctor?'

'I was, long before I boarded the Ark.'

She guided Shem to a vantage point that gave them a good view of the shattered ship.

'Can you see the medi-bay out there?'

Shem looked over the wreckage. It went on for miles. Squinting against the fires and smoke, he tried to see if there were people moving, but it was impossible.

Then he saw the bridge.

'I have to go there,' he said to the woman.

Painstakingly, Shem made his way down from the ledge. Once at ground level, he jogged to the bridge. He wanted to find the captain, someone who could tell them what to do. Put their lives in order.

When he reached the bridge, he found it was almost intact, having fared better than most places he had seen from above. But as he stepped inside, he saw the bodies of the bridge crew, broken and cold, their wide eyes staring at the sky.

'Dammit.'

With glassy eyes, Shem turned away and surveyed the landscape beyond. He saw fires, shattered bulkheads, destroyed furniture, and the occasional shock of red against grey. Bile rose in his throat as he thought about the thousands of people who had called the Ark home. He took a few steps through the bridge and saw a hand poking through the rubble. The fingers were twitching.

Shem flew into action, hoisting machine parts aside to reveal Garret. His face was bruised and bloody, his leg was sticking out at an unnatural angle, and he was unconscious. Shem called for help. He could feel a faint pulse in Garret's wrist – enough to fight for.

The older woman arrived beside him.

'I followed you. You seemed to know your way around the crew's quarters.'

She checked Garret over. 'Looks like a broken leg, severe head trauma, some third-degree burns and even a touch of frostbite on the extremities. They must've been exposed to the vacuum before falling through the atmosphere. He's lucky to be alive, but I suppose we all are. Without proper care, I don't expect him to survive.'

'We have to find the infirmary.' Shem stood up to find a group of six people standing in a little knot beside the bridge door.

'You!' He pointed. 'Build me something I can use as a stretcher. We're taking Garret with us.'

It took about half an hour but they eventually had a sheet of steel grid that dipped in the middle to cradle Garret's body, with some handles they had fashioned using fabric from their clothes.

All across the crash site, which stretched for half a mile in all directions, survivors were crawling free and wandering around, dazed and in search of help. They were looking for loved ones, calling out names and weeping over corpses. Here and there, two or more small groups would meet and become one; then they would find more people, the group snowballing across the debris, collecting the living and mourning the dead.

Shem found himself mixed in with a group of civilians and only one or two crew members. He recognised them as having worked with Ham. A girl called Lucy and a guy who went by the name of Zach, or something similar. They had always seemed to treat Ham well.

Eventually there were only really two large groups, traversing the wreck site towards each other. Alissa saw the group heading towards them. She had been holding onto Ham's hand throughout the last few hours, trying to keep him from breaking down.

'Hey, Alissa.'

She looked up at Ham as he spoke.

'Is that Shem?'

He pointed a finger at the approaching group, and one man who was limping towards them.

Without a second thought, Alissa began to run across the wasteland, never taking her eyes off her friend.

Shem saw the flash of brunette heading towards him at speed, and let out a laugh of sheer relief as he hobbled forward.

With open arms, Alissa flung herself at Shem and even through the pain, he caught her and held her close. After a moment or two, Shem whispered in her ear: 'What about Ham?'

Alissa pulled away and turned to her group, tears flowing freely down her cheeks.

'Ham! Get over here!' she called out. Ham stepped out and jogged over, wrapping them both in his massive arms.

'I was so scared, you guys.'

'It's not over, Ham.' Shem looked serious. 'There's no way we can fly out of here ...'

Alissa nodded and finished his thought. 'And there's a whole lot of aliens up there that are gonna want to see us all dead.'

Shem put his hand on her shoulder. 'There's something else. Garret is alive. But he's in pretty bad shape.'

He stepped aside as his own group caught up with them. Alissa saw Garret on the makeshift stretcher and her eyes widened.

'We have to get him to Megan. She's setting up an infirmary a short way from here.'

They all began to move, like a swarm of bees, heading in one direction across the burning landscape.

***

These were the survivors, the ones who would be remembered for living through the fall. Over the coming days, some of them would die from their extensive injuries and others would recover. But there was no way out for them now, no rescue, just an empty world and the remains of their ship. The Committee would come for them, to eradicate the survivors and destroy humanity once and for all. But when the time came, these humans would be ready. They would fight.

This would be their new world.

To be Concluded...

ACKNOWLEDGEMENTS

This story could not have happened without the help of the following people.

Ken Dalrymple, for your constant support.
Miblart, for the amazing cover art.
Mike Faulkner, for being a brilliant copy editor.

ABOUT THE AUTHOR

Jennifer Swift has been an avid science fiction fan for many years. Surrounding herself with books and TV shows that captured her imagination. From Star Trek to Red Dwarf, the idea of space travel has implanted itself deep within her mind, inspiring a series that not only stays true to science fiction, but offers an array of likeable and realistic characters that you can't help but become attached to.

Printed in Great Britain
by Amazon

67996884R00137